"If you don't mind, I'd rather go somewhere...a little more private."

"I don't think so," he said softly. "You've already had more than enough concessions. You've got your opportunity—which is precisely two minutes—to tell me what all this damned mystery is about." His mouth hardened. "And it had better be good."

Her voice was trembling, but somehow she got the words out. "Our meeting was very different from most you must encounter, Your Majesty— or at least I'm assuming it was. It was back in the summer nearly two years ago—in England—at a party during a tour of the Zaffirinthos marbles. In fact, we did more than meet. Much more. As it happens, we had a short affair, and as a consequence..." She saw the disbelief and the anger beginning to blaze from his amber eyes. "As a consequence I...I have a little son. Or rather *we* have a son. What I should say is...*you* have a son, Your Majesty."

All about the author...
Sharon Kendrick

When I was told off as a child for making up stories, little did I know that one day I'd earn my living by writing them!

To the horror of my parents, I left school at sixteen and did a bewildering variety of jobs. I was a London DJ (in the now-trendy Primrose Hill!), a decorator and a singer. After that I became a cook, a photographer and eventually a nurse. I waitressed in the south of France, drove an ambulance in Australia, saw lots of beautiful sights but could never settle down. Everywhere I went I felt like a square peg—until one day I started writing again and then everything just fell into place. I felt the way Cinderella must have done when the glass slipper fitted!

Today I have the best job in the world—writing passionate romances for Harlequin Books. I like writing stories that are sexy and fast paced, yet packed full of emotion—stories that readers will identify with, that will make them laugh and cry.

I live in Winchester, England, (one of the most stunning cities in the world; but don't take my word for it—come see for yourself!) and regularly visit London and Paris. Oh, and I love hearing from my readers all over the world...so I think it's over to you!

With warmest wishes,

Sharon Kendrick

www.sharonkendrick.com

Sharon Kendrick

HIS MAJESTY'S CHILD

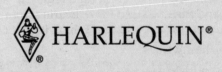

TORONTO • NEW YORK • LONDON
AMSTERDAM • PARIS • SYDNEY • HAMBURG
STOCKHOLM • ATHENS • TOKYO • MILAN • MADRID
PRAGUE • WARSAW • BUDAPEST • AUCKLAND

ISBN-13: 978-0-373-12972-0

HIS MAJESTY'S CHILD

Previously published in the U.K. under the title
THE ROYAL BABY REVELATION

First North American Publication 2011

Copyright © 2010 by Sharon Kendrick

HIS MAJESTY'S CHILD

This book is dedicated with love
to the mischievous and inspirational
Monica Black—whose talents as wife,
mother and raconteur are legendary.

CHAPTER ONE

GOLDEN light streamed down from the vaulted ceiling but Melissa didn't pay it any attention. Even palaces paled into insignificance when measured against the realisation that her moment had come.

At last.

Sometimes it seemed as if her life had been defined by this moment—and that her future would be determined by its outcome. A moment she could trace right back to that terrifying second when she'd held the strip of plastic in her shaking fingers and seen the unmistakable blue line which had confirmed her pregnancy.

And the world as she'd known it had changed for ever.

'Did you hear me, Melissa?' Stephen's voice punctured her ballooning thoughts. 'I said that the King will see you shortly.'

'Yes. Yes, I heard you,' said Melissa, her heart beginning to pound as she allowed herself a brief glance in one of the ornate mirrors which lined the ante-room of the Zaffirinthos palace. She was not a vain woman—there would have been no time for vanity in her life even if her looks had warranted it. She had the kind of face which wouldn't have launched even a single ship—let alone a thousand. But an audience with the King…

The King who had fathered her son!

As she tidied her long, thick hair for what felt the hundredth time she hoped she looked better from the outside than she felt on the inside. Because she had to look her best. Her very best. She had to make Casimiro believe that she was worth something. That she was fit to be the mother of his child. Smoothing damp palms down over the linen of her new dress, she looked anxiously to Stephen for some kind of confirmation. 'Do I…do I look okay?'

He flicked her a brief glance before returning his attention to the clipboard in his hand. 'You look fine—but you do realise he isn't going to notice what you're wearing? Royals never do. We're staff so we're deemed servants—and they never look properly at servants. We're just there—like part of the wallpaper.'

'Wallpaper,' she repeated blankly.

'That's right. Part of the background. All he wants from you is a brief outline of the itinerary for tonight's ball. Basically, I've told him everything he needs to know—but since you've organised the flowers and the band he wants to speak to you himself, to thank you. It's a courtesy thing. Keep it short and keep it sweet, and don't forget—only speak when you're spoken to.'

'Of course I won't forget.' There was a pause. What Melissa might have called a pregnant pause if the expression hadn't mocked her quite so much. 'You know I've…I've met the King once before,' she ventured.

Stephen frowned as he looked up from his clipboard. 'When?'

What *had* made her say that? Was it perhaps to pave the way for the number one dream scenario she'd nurtured for so long—that Casimiro would immediately acknowledge Ben as his son and heir? That she would be able to tell people about Ben's dad with a certain amount of pride, instead of biting her lip and saying that she'd rather not talk about it?

The only trouble with dream scenarios was that once you started coming up with them, it wasn't easy to stop.

Because wasn't it possible that the King might even be grateful to her for the bombshell she was about to drop—especially as his younger brother's wife had recently given birth to a son. The world's press had fanfared the birth of an heir to the fabulous Mediterranean kingdom, but Melissa knew that wasn't true. Because Ben was the heir. *The true heir.*

She cleared her throat. 'When…when we did that museum party in London, for the touring exhibition of the Zaffirinthos marbles. Casimiro was there—and at the after-show party. Surely you remember?'

'Sure I do.' Stephen screwed up his eyes. 'You helped me hand out the canapés that night, Mel—I doubt whether you actually engaged him in any conversation other than, "Would you like another hors d'oeuvre, Your Majesty?" And if you're expecting him to remember you from back then, you'd better think again.'

Melissa gave a brief, nervous smile. Of course her boss wouldn't have noticed—for there had been no chemistry or eye contact between the party planner's assistant and the eligible King during what had been just another glittering socialite gathering. You would hardly expect the guest of honour to engage in light-hearted banter with a woman who was there simply to serve the privileged throng.

And yet what would Stephen say if he knew just what the King *had* said to her the very next night when she had been cold and empty and aching for some human comfort? Something along the lines of how criminal it was for her to wear panties at all…and then he had proceeded to remove them with a dexterity which, when coupled with a passionate kiss, had made any argument against his love-making completely futile.

But Stephen was clearly oblivious to the fact that she had become intimate with the man who ruled the prosperous Mediterranean island of Zaffirinthos. He had no idea that Casimiro was Ben's father. In fact, neither did her aunt, who was looking after Ben back in England at this very moment. No one did—not even Casimiro himself. It was a terrible, aching secret she had been forced to keep to herself—but soon she would be free of the intolerable burden.

'And people are still concerned about the King's health, of course,' continued Stephen thoughtfully.

At this, Melissa stilled. 'He's…he's not ill?'

'Ill? He's the fittest man I've ever seen—which is a miracle when you stop to think about it,' said Stephen reflectively. 'You know he nearly died the year before last, don't you?'

Despite the warmth of the late-May evening, Melissa couldn't suppress the shiver which Stephen's words produced as they took her back to that terrible time. A time which had been like a living hell. Of course she knew that Casimiro had nearly died—hadn't she sat awake for hours watching the twenty-four hour news channel, wide-eyed and weary from lack of sleep as she'd waited for bulletins which had told her very little?

The King is fighting for his life had been the one grim and enduring announcement which had made her recognise that she couldn't keep burying her head in the sand.

And hadn't Casimiro's eventual recovery spurred her into action—slamming home the realisation that she must tell him about his baby? Even if she'd failed in her attempts to contact him before—because Kings were pretty much unreachable to people like her—this time she must. She *must*. For Ben was more than just a beautiful little boy she adored with all her heart—he was the progeny of a king; heir to a royal kingdom—and didn't they both have a right to know that?

'He...he fell off his horse, didn't he?' she questioned—a fact she already knew. Actually, about the *only* fact she knew about the accident—though perhaps Stephen could tell her more.

'Landed on his head—reckless fool. Was in a coma for weeks.'

'But he's all right now?'

'Apparently. Though one of his staff was indiscreet enough to tell me that the King's initial relief at his full recovery has given way to a cold demeanour which makes most of them quake.'

This was not what Melissa wanted to hear. She wanted to hear that Casimiro was the sunniest person on the planet. That he would smile on her with delight when she grabbed an opportune moment to tell him her earth-shattering news, and tell her that she wasn't to worry. That he would sort it all out.

'Cold?' she echoed.

'Positively icy.' Stephen laughed. 'So, like I say, Melissa—keep it short and keep it sweet.'

'I'll try to remember. See you in a while,' she said, and with strangely reluctant footsteps, she began to follow the footman who was waiting to lead her to the King's offices.

She'd only arrived at the palace yesterday—stepping off a private jet which had been light years away from her usual mode of public transport on crowded buses and trains. Ready to help Stephen with the final preparations for the ball that King Casimiro was throwing. It was to be a belated wedding party for his younger brother Xaviero and wife Catherine—as well as a celebration of the birth of their baby son. And Stephen was organising the gathering—these days he seemed to have a monopoly on high-profile events, and royal gatherings were his speciality.

Stephen Woods was her boss—she helped him plan his society parties, a job she'd stumbled on more by chance than by judgement. They'd met when Melissa had been temping in one of his offices—after she'd been forced to drop out of college due to a lack of funds when her mother had died. In the midst of her grief, Stephen had recognised her talent and made her feel as if she was worth something. Time and time again, the flamboyant caterer had told Melissa that her artistic eye was invaluable to him. That her talent for transforming the mundane into something extraordinary was what helped get his business talked about and her behind-the-scenes work was second to none. Which was why he valued her enough to let her choose her own hours and to work them around Ben—and she was so grateful to him for that.

Lost in thought, Melissa barely noticed the splendour and dimensions of the magnificent palace as she followed the footman along the wide marble corridors. The paintings on the walls seemed to all blur into one and the statues of ancient gods and goddesses bathed in sunlight were completely lost on her. She just kept thinking about Ben—and how his life was about to take on an entirely new direction. Very soon he would have a father at long last—a father he could grow to know and to love. Someone who would be able to enrich his young life with all kinds of benefits.

Eventually coming to a halt, the footman knocked loudly on an ornate pair of doors and she heard a single terse word emanating from within.

'*Sí?*'

There wasn't really time to register the throaty and sexy accent—which she knew spoke Greek as fluently as Italian—or the fact that she was seconds away from seeing him, because the doors were pushed open. Melissa's hands were trembling as she was summoned inside—indeed it seemed as if her whole body was trembling. The thought that her most longed-for wish was about to come true was making her wonder whether her shaky legs would bear her weight—but she knew that she had to stay calm and focused. She *had* to.

And then she saw him.

Seated at his desk with an air of intense concentration as he scrutinised a sheaf of papers which were spread out in front of him, he seemed to have been carved from a piece of dark and glittering stone and was completely oblivious to her presence. For a moment, she just stood there—drinking him in. The ebony sheen of his hair and the powerful broad shoulders set her pulse racing. He might have been born to rule with untold riches at his clever fingertips, but to Melissa he had always been the most perfect man she'd ever seen, and, from this angle, that much hadn't changed.

Suddenly, he looked up and her heart lurched with excited recognition as their eyes met—for, despite everything, she felt her heart turn over with longing. Because what woman wouldn't feel moved by the sight of her ex-lover whose seed had grown inside her belly for nine long months? Time after time he'd preoccupied her thoughts—even if he'd never shown the slightest inclination to stay in touch with her. How long had it been since she'd seen him? she wondered dazedly. Getting on for two years. *Nearly two whole years!*

She stared into deep amber eyes fringed with jet-dark lashes, which made his gaze seem to pierce right through her. At hair the colour of a raven's wing. At autocratic and proud features and a lean, muscular body, which was wearing some kind of uniform. Casimiro. It was Casimiro—but he seemed so different. His face seemed darker, harder—more forbidding than she remembered it. She swallowed. Cloaked in the unmistakable aura of royalty, he looked regal and imposing—and utterly, utterly inaccessible.

Yet once he had been accessible, hadn't he? she reminded herself. Accessible enough to take you to his bed and to thrust his golden-dark body into yours over and over again. It was just seeing him now—sitting in his very own palace—that Melissa felt insecurity wash over her. Because even though you knew something intellectually, you couldn't always accept it—not emotionally. But now, for the first time, she did. He really *was* a king. A king who ruled an exquisite island kingdom. Who was lord and master of all he surveyed. And the enormity of what lay before her seemed positively daunting.

But it was too late to back out now—the access she had longed for had finally been granted—and with a fast-thudding heart, Melissa smiled. Because he was the father of her child and—no matter what had happened in the past—surely they could be adult about the future?

She hadn't exactly expected him to leap to his feet with pleasure and to pull her into his arms, but she had been expecting him to say *something*. To have registered *some* kind of emotion on his face—like shock or surprise, maybe even dismay, because she wasn't naïve enough not to realise that his life would have moved on in all kinds of ways. But his countenance remained cold—as cold as ice—and maybe it was up to her to break it.

Fixing a hopeful look to her face, she attempted a smile. 'H-hello,' she said, even though the word felt like a pebble which had stuck in her throat.

For a moment, Casimiro did not respond to her greeting or to her soft English accent. He had been so deep in troubled thought that he could barely remember summoning anyone to his offices, and now he narrowed his eyes as he studied the woman who stood before him.

Her long, glossy hair was the colour of strong tea—the brown hair which was so widespread among Englishwomen—and her eyes were green. Skin so pale it was almost translucent showed a fine tracery of blue veins at her temples and she wore a dress whose only eye-catching feature was the fact that it drew his attention to a pair of long and very attractive legs.

He frowned. All his life had been steeped in protocol—it was as much a part of his existence as breathing itself. Often he professed himself bored with such etiquette and railed against its restrictions—but its absence was enough to ensure his frosty disapproval. Placing his gold fountain pen down on the desk, he fixed her with a look of chilly censure.

'And you are...?' he questioned coldly.

Melissa's smile slipped by a fraction and she was taken aback by his unfriendliness. Was this some kind of joke? She met amber eyes—but amber was supposed to be warm and glowing, wasn't it? Not like the glance which was searing its way through her. This was cold, impenetrable—hard and unwelcoming. Heart thundering, she searched his aristocratic features for some kind of recognition. Some vague stirring of memory. Some acknowledgement that this was a woman he had made love to over and over again.

But there was nothing on his face other than a faintly dismissive stare and, slowly, the unbelievable began to dawn on her protesting mind.

He doesn't know who you are!

For a moment she didn't believe it. Thought that he might be playing some kind of cruel game with her—but his demeanour remained hard and obdurate, and surely nobody could be *that* good an actor?

Yes, their affair had lasted only a few short days— but surely she wasn't completely forgettable? In fact, hadn't he told her that he would always remember their passionate encounter? Had he been lying when he'd said that—or was it just a line he'd spun to countless women, despite having had the ability to make her feel so intensely special at the time?

Eyes blinking rapidly, Melissa tried to put her jumbled thoughts into some semblance of order. Forcing herself not to do something crazy, that afterwards she might regret. Like blurting something out. Something along the lines of: *Your Royal Highness, I can see my son's face in your features. Or I have a miniature version of you back home, Casimiro—an heir you aren't even aware of.*

But she couldn't possibly do that. Not right out of the blue. Not when she'd already decided that she was going to have to choose her moment to tell him very carefully. And standing beneath the near-contemptuous gaze of a man who was regarding her as if she'd tumbled down from space and were burning an unwelcome hole in his priceless silk rug would never be described as ideal, not in anyone's eyes.

'I'm Melissa,' she said, hoping against hope that the sound of her Christian name might stir something in his memory. Didn't he once say that it made him think of honey?

'Melissa?'

'Melissa Maguire.'

He flicked her a look of barely restrained boredom. 'I'm none the wiser.'

What could she say which might jog his memory? Some half-forgotten fragment of conversation which might have stayed alive in his mind even if the memory of her eager love-making didn't. Hadn't he told her that the afternoon when they'd sneaked out on the little river boat had been one of the best of his life? Swallowing down her hurt, she wobbled him a smile. 'I live…I live just outside London in a place called Walton-on-Thames. Not far from the river, where you can hire rowing boats. You might—'

'I might be in danger of falling asleep any minute now if you continue with your dull little monologue.' Amber eyes iced through her as he cut into her faltering words. 'I didn't ask for your life story. I asked what you're doing here, waltzing into my private rooms with a complete and utter lack of regard.' He paused as all the frustration and uncertainty of the past months now found a legitimate outlet for his intense irritation. 'Because I'm assuming that you know who *I* am—even though you have made no suitable acknowlededgment of the fact.'

'Of course I know who you are,' she said quickly. 'You are the King of Zaffirinthos.'

'And yet you greet me as you would a casual friend. You do not lower your eyes in deference? Nor attempt the curtsey which my title merits?'

Melissa heard the silky barbs which spiked his icy request and shakily she attempted to comply—but it felt like a form of humiliation as she crossed one ankle behind the other and awkwardly dipped her knees, like some sort of adolescent frog. Inside she felt upset and angry—his sardonic comments coming hot on the heels of the realisation that he didn't recognise her. Why *should* she have to bow and scrape to him—when she was the mother of his child?

Yet now was probably not the best time to exhibit rebellion and so she executed the most graceful curtsey she could manage—which wasn't easy given that she was now feeling hot and flustered and her linen dress didn't allow for much movement. 'Forgive me, Your Highness,' she said.

'Majesty,' he corrected silkily—although the irony of his statement did not escape him. Not His Majesty for very much longer, he thought—with a heart which grew heavy at the thought of what lay ahead. Soon he would be free of all the accoutrements which had turned his life into a gilded cage. When he made his dramatic announcement at the ball that night, it would put an end at last to all the speculation about his future.

But as he studied the top of the Englishwoman's bent head Casimiro's intuition was alerted—something that had not been lost as a result of his accident, although he had been robbed of much else. There was something about her behaviour which didn't add up—something about her attitude which didn't make sense—though he couldn't for the life of him put his finger on what it could be.

'Get up,' he ordered impatiently.

Feeling the hot prickle of sweat between her breasts, Melissa rose and lifted her eyes to his. 'Yes, Your Majesty.'

'Why are you here?' he demanded softly.

'You sent for me.'

Had he? In truth, his mind had been so caught up with the enormous step he was about to take. The new journey he was about to embark on had preoccupied so much of his thinking that he had barely given a thought to the running of the palace. He glanced down quickly at the papers on his desk, straightening them into a neat pile before fixing her with a cool stare. 'Very well—then justify my command. Remind me who you are and what you do.'

It was possibly the most insulting way he could have reinforced her lack of status, but Melissa was determined that he would not see how much it had hurt. What good would *that* do? Make him see you as a person, rather than a hindrance. Give him the facts. The facts behind your *real* motive for being here. From somewhere, she found the glimmer of a professional smile.

'I work for Stephen Woods, the party planner, Your Majesty. I've been helping to arrange the ball from back in England. I arrived yesterday to help with the finishing touches and he told me…Stephen, that is…that I was to give you a brief itinerary of tonight's events.' She hesitated. He had also said that the King wanted to thank her—but somehow she didn't think that was going to happen.

'Did he?' Casimiro's eyes narrowed thoughtfully. 'Well, in that case—you'd better go ahead. Sit down,' he ordered carelessly.

'Thank you.' Praying for her breathing to return to something approaching normality, Melissa slid into the delicate-looking gilt chair he had indicated on the other side of his desk.

'So,' he drawled. 'Talk me through it.'

With the tip of her tongue, Melissa moistened her dry lips, trying not to feel self-conscious—though she was acutely aware of his moody and handsome face as the dark golden gaze arrowed into her. How the hell was he going to react when she told him? And just when *was* she going to tell him?

She gave herself a moment's grace. Everyone's life was measured by moments, she realised—but maybe this was an important one, too. Maybe this was the time to impress him with her efficiency and work-ethic rather than come right out and tell him he was a daddy.

'The ball will start at eight—with your entrance, Your Majesty. That will be followed by the arrival of your brother—the Prince Xaviero, his wife, Princess Catherine—and their baby son, the Prince Cosimo.'

'Is it not too late for the infant Prince to be awake?' he bit out.

'Well, maybe just a little.' She cleared her throat. 'It's just…well, we thought that this might be a good opportunity to allow for a photo opportunity, Your Majesty. Since this is a belated wedding party and christening celebration all rolled into one, we've been inundated with requests for shots of the new Prince with his mother and father.' She paused. 'And if you give the press their shots, afterwards they'll hopefully leave you alone.'

He narrowed his eyes as he listened to her, knowing that she was only expressing the fundamental truth of the situation. Along with his own people, the world was already half in love with his little nephew—for a royal baby captured the collective imagination as little else did. In truth, he couldn't blame them—not just because the child was cute, but because his lusty new life promised so much.

Didn't the infant Cosimo symbolise hope for the future—and the continuity of one of the oldest royal bloodlines in Europe? And hadn't his birth increased the pressure on Casimiro to find himself a bride and to produce a child of his own?

His mouth hardened. Well, he would not play ball. Not any more. He had followed orders all his life and he would certainly not procreate to order. If the past months had taught him anything, it was that he could no longer continue with this way of living. He had all the trappings that most men lusted after, but they were called *trappings* for a reason—they tied you down and constrained you with their golden snare, and he wanted to break free from them once and for all.

Deep in his veins ran a restlessness which had been even more pronounced since the accident and a restless king could not be a good king. Casimiro's mouth tightened. And there was another reason behind his proposed plan. Something else which had haunted him ever since he had awoken from his coma...

'Would you have any objections to that, Your Majesty?'

Her soft accent cut into his thoughts and he looked at her with his eyebrows raised. 'What?'

'A supervised photo-call with your brother and his family?' she continued smoothly.

'Objections?' He gave a short and bitter laugh as her question broke into his troubled thoughts. 'At least a hundred—and then a hundred more—but I can see the sense behind your words. Speak to my people about security,' he ordered. 'And ensure they don't run over time—because they'll try their damnedest. Too much flash photography is not good for a small child. Not particularly good for adults either,' he added on a sardonic aside as he met her eyes with a look which was resigned, rather than interested. 'What next?'

'Dinner for two hundred. And your brother is making

a short speech afterwards to thank you for throwing the party. Then the fireworks. After that—'

'Wait.' His peremptory request silenced her and he was surprised by the stone-like feeling deep in his heart. 'I wish to make a speech myself,' he said heavily. 'Before my brother.'

Melissa sat up in alarm. 'But, Your Majesty—'

His eyes glittered dangerously. 'What?'

She thought about the foreign royal families, the dignitaries and the glitterati who were arriving from mainland Europe and from the United States, the security services who were already working to the tightest of schedules, and she drew a deep breath. Surely he couldn't spring something like this on her at the last minute which would throw all her plans out? 'The timetable has been worked out down to the last second.'

'Then damned well *un*work it,' he drawled unhelpfully. 'Isn't that what you're being paid for?'

Again, his cutting words drummed in her lack of status—but somehow Melissa kept the hurt from registering on her face.

'Very well, Your Majesty—if…if you can let me know how long you need to say your piece, then I'll work it into the schedule and inform everybody of the change. It can…it can all be sorted out, I'm sure.'

Aware that her words were stumbling out of her lips like some sort of plea, she searched his face in a last-ditch attempt to strike a chord of recognition. *Remember me*, she urged him silently as she leaned forward by a fraction. *Remember who I am. Remember you said I was sweeter than honey. That my skin was softer than a cloud. Don't you remember the way that you buried your*

*mouth against my neck and moaned out your pleasure
while you were deep inside me?*

Casimiro frowned at her reaction as something intangible seemed to shimmer through the air towards him.
Her green eyes had suddenly grown as dark as the lunar
eclipse and her lips had parted in a way which made
them look almost kissable. *Very* kissable, in fact. And
suddenly he caught a drift of her perfume as she moved.
Some subtle scent of lilac which seemed to pervade the
very air with its delicacy—and for a moment he stilled,
as if somebody had turned him to stone.

He felt something nudging insistently at the corners
of his mind—what the hell had that smell reminded him
of? But then, like a delicious dream disturbed by a loud
noise, it was gone, and no amount of concentration could
get it back again.

Silently, he cursed as he stared at her and glimpsed
the faint gleam of her tongue through her half-opened
mouth. And inexplicably, he felt a swift, sharp hardening
at his groin—a tumescent ridge which was heating his
blood and making his senses start fizzing with desire. So
that for one insane moment he thought about pulling her
into his arms—of raking his fingers through that thick
brown hair and tilting up her face before ravishing those
quivering lips of hers.

Angrily, he gave a little click of irritation. What the
hell was he thinking of? This was some itinerant little
worker from England—not a woman worthy of his
desire. And, yes, it was an age since he had lost himself
in the incomparable pleasures of sex—not since before
his accident, that was for sure. Was he so frustrated that
he was allowing desperation to cloud his judgement—he

who could have any woman he wanted? And *would* have, he vowed silently.

At tonight's ball, there would be a surplus of women just longing for him to notice them—among them would-be brides from all the most aristocratic families in the world. But he was not looking for a bride. He was looking for a lover—a lover who would take whatever he was prepared to offer.

There would be plenty of those kinds of women there too, he thought—with a grim kind of satisfaction. The most beautiful women which nature had to offer would be eying him with predatory eyes and eager bodies. Casimiro's mouth hardened as he willed his unwanted erection to subside.

It was time to break his self-imposed sexual drought—and to lose himself in the mindless pleasures of the body before he embarked on his self-imposed exile. And when he *did*—when he surrendered to sex again—it would be with someone far more worthy of his affections than this tall Englishwoman with her strangely intense attitude. The sooner he could start choosing his own company—instead of having it forced upon him by his position—the better.

He realised that she was still sitting there, staring at him as if she had every right to linger in the King's private offices. 'I think we've covered everything, don't you?' he said.

His curt words were clearly a dismissal—but just in case she hadn't got the message the double-doors opened at precisely that moment. He must have rung some kind of secret bell—or maybe she had just used up her allotted time with him. And this time it wasn't a footman who stood there, but one of his aides—a hard-faced man who flicked her a hostile glance which left her in no doubt that she had overstayed her welcome.

'*Majesty?*' the man said.

'Ah, Orso,' said Casimiro. 'Signorina Maguire is just going. See her out, will you?'

'*Certo, Majesty.*' Orso gestured towards the door, giving Melissa no choice but to leave—her cheeks burning as she scrambled to her feet.

She glanced at the King but he was studying something on his desk—as though he'd forgotten she was there. *As though she'd never been there at all.* Self-consciously, she walked past the aide—realising that she'd thrown away the perfect opportunity to tell the King about his son.

And wondering when on earth she was going to get another one.

CHAPTER TWO

AFTER the Englishwoman had gone, Casimiro sat perfectly still for a moment before picking up the document which lay on the desk before him, detailing possibly the most important speech of his life. A speech which even Orso—his closest aide for many years—remained in complete ignorance of.

The speech which spelt out his abdication announcement.

Swallowing down the sudden wave of emotion which rose in his throat, he got to his feet and walked over to the huge windows, looking out at the palace gardens. What a view! Roses and oranges and cool, flowing fountains and, beyond that, the sea. He had known this view since boyhood—had been brought into this suite of offices from infancy—for his father had believed in his son and heir being schooled for the monarchy from the very outset. There were even photographs of him in the palace archives—as a little toddler crawling around beneath the enormous desk while his father had signed the Treaty Of Rhodes.

Then, when his beloved mother had succumbed to the brain haemorrhage which had eventually killed her, his father had devoted most of his time and energy to teaching his son about the responsibilities and the privileges of being King. Often Casimiro suspected that his brother Xaviero had felt left out—the neglected younger son badly missing the mother he had been so close to. Grief hadn't really been discussed in those days—especially not among high-born royals—so that both boys had suffered essentially lonely childhoods.

But Casimiro had never questioned his destiny—indeed, he had seized it with enthusiastic and modernising hands. He had embraced all that he could do for his beloved Zaffirinthos—and joyfully set into motion a whole raft of reforms which had made the people of his Mediterranean island more prosperous and contented than ever before. Yet along with his success as ruler had come the bitter realisation of how much this job demanded. How it ate into the rest of your life and devoured it like an ever-hungry predator. Disillusion had begun to gnaw away at him and made him long to be free.

But there was another reason why he knew he must step down from the throne—for the accident which had almost felled him had left behind a dark legacy. Unknown to anyone, there was a small but terrifying gap in his memory as a result of his near-fatal fall. Fierce pride and a determination that a king should never show weakness in front of his court or his people had meant that Casimiro had successfully concealed the fact from the world. Not even his doctors had guessed—even though at times he felt as if he were walking on a knife-edge. At times he felt guilty at the subterfuge and at others he was overwhelmed with frustration by his lack of recall.

But there *was* a solution—and a heartbreakingly simple one. It was time to pass on the royal reins to the brother who had always secretly lusted after his role as King—the brother who came with his own ready-made heir. Xaviero would become King; it was time for Casimiro to go.

And tonight he would make that announcement to the world.

Glancing at his watch, Casimiro locked away his papers and then walked briskly to the thankful solitude of his state apartments where he stripped and stood beneath the powerful jets of the shower. But while soaping the hard contours of his body, he felt a sudden fierce wave of desire spring to his manhood.

Closing his eyes, he willed the image to subside. For what good was desire unless you had a woman with you? Surely that was like looking at the sea from behind a window—instead of getting out there and enjoying the toss and spin of the waves for yourself?

For one brief moment he thought of the Englishwoman who had been in his office earlier—recalling the strangely evocative scent of lilac and the provocative gleam of her lips—and he felt his hand begin to stray towards his groin…but only for a second. Instead, he turned the tap as icy shower jets killed his desire and focused his mind on the enormity of what lay ahead.

Refreshed and glowing, he dressed in a dark and formal suit and slipped the speech into the pocket of his jacket. And at eight o' clock on the dot Casimiro walked into the ballroom to a fanfare of trumpets, with Orso and his other aides surrounding him like a satellite of small suns around a giant planet. A smattering of applause greeted his entrance and he was aware of the intense scent of flowers and the frantic guttering of hundreds of tall, white candles.

All eyes were upon him—every woman decked in precious gems worn with designer gowns which held their gym-perfect bodies to their best advantage, because even if they were married there was no greater accolade than to be looked on with approval by the King of Zaffirinthos. And most of them would have begged to be his lover if he'd only deigned to click his careless fingers in their direction.

But Casimiro was aware of a pair of eyes burning into him. A pair of eyes which were startlingly green— their expression fierce and intent as the Englishwoman who had come to his study earlier now stared at him from across the ballroom. On her face was a look he could never remember seeing before—and novelty was rare enough to command his attention, even though the import of what he was about to do tonight hung like the sword of Damocles above his head.

More trumpets sounded and announced the entrance of the infant Prince and huge cheers went up round the ballroom. Yet Casimiro saw that the Englishwoman's attention was still fixed firmly to him when everyone else was vying for a glimpse of the baby. He should have been irritated at yet another shocking lack of protocol and yet, intriguingly, she had captured his attention. Maybe it was a kind of distraction technique to take his mind off what lay ahead, but he found himself studying her back with an intensity which her appearance did not merit—certainly not when you compared her to the other women in the room.

The dress she wore tonight covered the long legs which had briefly captured his attention earlier. Plain black and silky, the long gown rippled to the ground from a fairly modest scooped neckline and yet, curiously, she drew the eye *because* she was so understated.

Well, of course she is understated, he told himself as he saw the banks of cameras lining up like hunters in front of the baby Prince—*she's a member of staff.* It was like seeing a lump of bread and cheese set down at a lavish banquet—sometimes the commonplace had its own inexplicable power to capture the attention.

But as her gaze burned into him Casimiro felt the vaguest stirring of disquiet. As if someone had tugged at the invisible cord in his mind.

Despite a complete lack of appetite, he endured the overlong banquet with equanimity—though course after exquisite course of the finest produce failed to interest him, and neither did the princess seated next to him who was attempting to flirt with him. Increasingly, Casimiro could feel the darkness creeping over his heart and the only distraction to his troubled thoughts was the sight of the Englishwoman who stood in a discreet alcove at the other end of the banqueting hall—her eyes fixed intently on him every time he looked up.

He was used to being looked at by women—though rarely with such outrageous blatancy—but even he was surprised by her tenacious adoration. How on earth had she survived in her job so long? he wondered idly. Did she not realise that it was discourteous in the extreme to stare so openly at the monarch?

He found himself speculating on how much he might miss some areas of protocol when, to his astonishment, he saw her begin to weave her way through the glittering tables towards him—the almost shy look of resolve on her face making it abundantly clear that he, the King, was her target.

He frowned. Did she think that their brief interview had given her the right of access? Did she imagine that she was free to speak to him any time she liked?

Out of the corner of his eye, he saw Orso stir—his muscle-packed frame as imposing as the bear after which he'd been named. Yet he moved with surprising agility to speak softly into Casimiro's ear.

'Shall I get rid of her, Majesty?' he questioned, in the Greek in which both men were fluent and which was less widely understood than their first language of Italian.

Casimiro's instinctive response was to say yes as etiquette demanded—but as the woman called Melissa drew nearer her unquestionable breach of protocol was enough to again capture his interest. And something written on her face struck at a chord within him—an echo of the expression he had seen there earlier. Something which set off some far-distant warning bell ringing deep inside him.

Instinct told him to speak to her—and now that he was about to cast off the strictures of royal life, then surely he could listen to his instincts at long last. Surely he could satisfy his curiosity about what she wanted—if only as a distraction until this interminable meal ended, when the speech was burning a hole in his pocket and, unexpectedly, his heart was aching at the thought of delivering it.

'No. Let her speak. She intrigues me. Perhaps there is some problem to which she wishes to alert me. This ball *is* part of my gift to my brother and therefore my responsibility, after all.'

'But, Majesty—'

'Let her approach, Orso—but guide her more discreetly. All eyes are upon her and she has neither the poise nor the beauty to withstand such scrutiny.'

'*Ochi*, Majesty.'

Melissa walked towards the King, her heart crashing madly against her chest, feeling a rivulet of sweat beginning to trickle its way down between her breasts. She was scarcely able to believe that she was actually going through with this, but as she had been getting ready for tonight she'd realised that she couldn't delay telling him. Not for a moment longer. She had blown her opportunity when they'd been alone together earlier—sheer nerves had defeated her, along with her stupid and over-optimistic plan of waiting for the 'right' time. And there never was going to be a 'right' time—not when the situation was as wrong as could be. Even she, guided by fierce maternal love, could see that.

She had thought about delaying it until after the King's speech—but surely she wouldn't stand a chance of getting near him *then*? Not with people clamouring around to tell him how wonderful he was as they inevitably would.

She saw the towering form of his aide beginning to advance towards her with grim intent in his black eyes and she wondered if he had been told to act as a buffer between them. So that for one crazy moment, she actually thought of making a run for it. Of flying straight over to the King and blurting out her secret before anyone could stop her. But the man he had called Orso was lighter on his feet than his huge frame suggested—and suddenly he was by her side, with a light but iron-firm grip to her elbow which meant she was going nowhere without his say-so, and she felt her nerve begin to desert her.

'You wish to speak to the King?'

'Y-yes.'

'About *what*?' snapped Orso.

Meeting the glare from his eyes, Melissa knew it was imperative that she held her nerve. She had come this far and she would not be fobbed off with a member of his entourage. 'That's between me and the King. I wish to speak privately with him.'

'Then you will approach His Majesty with more caution.' Orso's heavily accented voice was harsh with disapproval. 'Unless you wish for a posse of his armed guards to spring on you and to throw you in the jailhouse at Ghalazamba?'

'Of c-course I don't,' she stumbled, some of her nerve deserting her.

'Then walk with me,' instructed Orso tersely.

He led her by a circuitous route to the long dais where Casimiro sat along with the other exulted guests. Melissa stood looking at the backs of them all—at the women's jewel-encrusted necklaces and priceless earrings which dangled down to their naked shoulders—and there was a moment when she wondered if he'd forgotten she was there. Until suddenly he turned, fastening her in the amber snare of his eyes—the faintest inclination of his dark head the only outward sign that he was summoning her towards him.

Heart crashing, she approached him. Had anyone

noticed that she wasn't busying herself on the sidelines with Stephen—helping deal with every little crisis as it arose? Which was what she *should* have been doing. But Melissa didn't care. It didn't even matter if her job was on the line. She could always find another job—but never find another father for her son.

'You are very impertinent,' Casimiro mused as she grew close enough to hear the whispered disapproval in his voice. 'To stare at me as the hyena regards the glistening flesh.'

Had she come over as *predatory*? 'I don't mean to be, Your Majesty.'

Again, he detected the faint drift of lilac as she leaned towards him. The sense of something tantalisingly close—like a wave which washed against the shoreline before retreating again. He frowned, his interest unexpectedly awakened. 'Do you always behave this way at functions?'

She wanted to say no—but hadn't she been pretty unprofessional the *last* time she'd met him? Yet *he* had been the one who had driven it, she reminded herself. Who had started this whole thing between them. And was she really so invisible—so inconsequential—that he couldn't remember a single thing about her or anything they'd done together?

'This is not the way I normally behave, no. Perhaps… perhaps it's the effect you have on me, Your Majesty.'

'I *beg* your pardon?'

'You don't remember, do you?' she whispered.

Sabre-sharp, her words sliced through him as she found his Achilles heel and Casimiro stilled. 'Remember *what*?' he bit out.

Was she going to have to spell it out for him? Was she really so unforgettable that he *still* didn't remember their affair? Staring at the august presence in front of her, Melissa allowed herself the bittersweet luxury of recall, remembering the night she'd first laid eyes on him.

It had been when London's biggest museum had exhibited the fabulous statues excavated during an archaeological dig on the island of Zaffirinthos. The aftershow party had been held at the house of a minor British royal—a magnificent mansion which had overlooked Green Park itself.

What had made the evening stand out had been the presence of the King of Zaffirinthos, who had flown in especially to witness the first stage of the international tour of the statues. And he had turned out to be an attraction who had proved even more newsworthy than the precious artefacts. An outrageously gorgeous man in his early thirties, he was quickly dubbed by the press: "The Most Eligible Man In Europe."

Melissa's first glimpse of the royal had certainly borne out all the hype. As he'd been shown around the museum for a private view of the show she could see why his face had been raved about in all the gossip columns and why every hostess in the capital was clamouring to get him onto her guest list.

It was an amazing face—all carved aristocratic features and skin which gleamed like gold. His eyes were golden too, a deeper, darker shade which was closer to amber—and the jet-dark waves of his hair looked as if they had been swirled onto his head with the bold brush-strokes of some master artist's charcoal pencil.

Why, with his powerful presence she had found herself thinking that he looked almost like a statue himself.

But the stillness of his muscular body did nothing to deflect the fact that he had about him some nebulous quality which transcended his royal status. Melissa felt there was something rather wild and *untamed* about him.

And, of course, she hadn't spoken to him. She had been too busy supervising the mass of summer flowers which had garlanded the entrance to the grand house in an attempt to detract from the unseasonably heavy rain outside—and reporting back to her hostess, who was a particularly exacting woman.

The evening had been memorable for another reason, too—the one which could always activate the dark aching hole inside her: the anniversary of her mother's death in that terrible car crash. Melissa knew it was slightly pathetic for a young adult like herself to describe herself as an orphan, but on this one night of the year—when she relived the terror of the midnight phone-call and the subsequent horror which had unfolded in the intensive care ward—that was exactly what she felt like.

She had put her emotions on hold until the end of the evening when she had been unable to stem the tide of tears any longer and in a cloakroom in a deserted part of the basement she had lost the battle, and given into quiet sobs of sorrow.

Eventually, emerging red-eyed into the corridor which led back up to the main part of the house, she had almost cannoned into a tall man—quickly turning her face to one side, too embarrassed to be seen by anyone in such a fragile state as she had tried to avoid him.

'Hey,' came a silken voice whose marked accent should have alerted her but she was so busy dabbing at her eyes with a crumpled-up tissue that she failed to make the connection. 'What's the rush?'

'Go away.' Melissa gulped and the moment she'd said it she realised just who he was and stared up at him in horror.

He looked as if he hadn't quite decided to be irritated or bemused—as if he wasn't used to people saying that to him. And then his eyes drifted over her and Melissa wondered how vile she must look with her shiny red nose and blotchy skin.

'You've been crying,' he observed, with the air of a man who was never cried in front of.

Ten out of ten for observation, she thought miserably—hating feeling so vulnerable and so awful in front of someone like him. 'Yes, I have,' she said, in a small voice, wondering why he wasn't upstairs drinking his champagne with the rest of the privileged gathering.

'Why?'

'It doesn't matter.'

'Oh, but it does—because I want to know. Don't you realise that I am a king?' His amber eyes glittered, his lips curving into a mocking smile. 'And that everything I command is always granted?'

For a moment she thought he was joking—and maybe he was, just a little. But she could also see that he expected an answer from her and so, with a sudden mulishness, Melissa decided to tell him. *Then* let him be sorry he had asked.

'It's the anniversary of my mother's death.'

There was a pause. 'Oh.'

She could see the sudden tightening of his face. Could hear the sudden chatter of conversation as a distant door was opened and the dull background patter of rain as it lashed against one of the basement doors. Perhaps he heard it too for she caught him looking down at her cheap shoes, and frowning—as if it had suddenly occurred to him that they might let in water.

'You want a ride home?' he questioned.

'From *you*?'

'Who else? You have a car waiting? A boyfriend perhaps?'

Suspiciously, she screwed up her eyes as if to check that he wasn't being sarcastic. 'No. I don't.'

'Then how were you planning on getting home?'

'On the underground.'

'Well, don't. I'll be outside. Don't keep me waiting.'

He walked off, leaving Melissa staring at him as if she'd seen a ghost. A ghost that looked and sounded like a king and had offered her a ride home. As she gave the kitchen a last minute check and changed from her black working dress into a pair of jeans and a raincoat she kept wondering whether she'd imagined the whole thing.

But she hadn't. A dark-tinted limousine was sitting a little way down the road and as her steps slowed uncertainly a chauffeur suddenly got out and opened the door for her.

Briefly, it occurred to her that this was the kind of action those real-life crime programmes you saw on TV always advised you against taking. She could see

Casimiro sitting in the back seat and when Melissa hesitated, this seemed to amuse him.

'So, are you getting in—or staying there and getting wet?'

Still she hesitated.

'Or perhaps you think I will leap on you? That you are completely irresistible to me?'

Melissa swallowed. Now he *was* being sarcastic. And suddenly she didn't care—not about whether it was right or wrong or the fact that he was a king. When compared to the bigger picture of mortality and the fact that she would never see her mother again—this was about as important as chicken-feed.

'Why are you doing this?' she questioned as she climbed into the back of the car and into his world of luxury and soft leather. 'Because you feel sorry for me?''

There was a pause, and then a fierce look came over his face—a look so dark and so bleak that Melissa felt as if she was intruding just by witnessing it. As if she had glimpsed into some dark corner of his soul.

'Because I know how hard it can be,' he said unexpectedly. 'To lose a mother.'

And that had been it, really. Two people brought together by a rainy night and a moment of empathy. Something had fused between them—bringing together a pair of lives which couldn't have been more disparate. Against all the odds, they had become lovers.

With lazy amusement, Casimiro told her that his usual aide was not accompanying him—and it seemed to amuse him to give the others the slip as often as possible. For five days he played hide-and-seek with them—ensuring just enough freedom to snatch at a life which could never be his, while reassuring the people who guarded him that he was safe. It seemed that everything the King did, he did well—if recklessly—and he embraced his new-found anonymity with a skill which would have made the finest actor turn green with envy.

In Melissa's tiny bedsit he—a man who had been fed every delicacy since birth—sampled beans on toast for the first time in his life. He drank cheap wine and made tea in a mug. The two of them hired a little boat on the river and he rode on the top deck of a red London bus without anyone knowing it was him. And they spent afternoons in bed, listening to the distant hum of traffic and the sound of their own heartbeats. He told her that she smelt of summer flowers and that her eyes were like emerald stars—and hadn't she just revelled in those lazy compliments?

Of course, it was over almost as soon as it began. Melissa had known that was going to happen—and Casimiro had never pretended that it was ever going to be otherwise. Five days could simultaneously feel like a moment or a lifetime, she discovered.

"You knew that this was never destined to last, didn't you?" he'd murmured on that last time in bed, his clever, seeking fingers trickling down over her belly to bury themselves in the soft fuzz of hair which lay at the fork of her thighs.

"Of course I did!" she'd whispered, praying that her voice wouldn't break down.

That didn't stop it hurting, of course, and the pain she felt was in direct proportion to her earlier joy—fierce and strong and almost unbearable. But somehow she managed to keep the tears at bay until they'd said their goodbyes—and once he'd gone she experienced an empty void, a kind of aching no-man's-land, before her world was completely shattered...

'Remember *what*?'

Casimiro's harsh question broke into her painful thoughts and Melissa felt her body jerk as the memories cleared and she found herself back in the present, standing beneath the imperious gaze of the man with the amber eyes in a banqueting hall full of the world's movers and shakers. But this was no longer the anonymous lover who had kissed her so passionately in her little bedsit—but a distant and remote stranger sitting on his kingly dais.

She met the icy question in his eyes. 'We've...we've met before, Your Majesty.'

'And?'

Melissa blinked, confused now. 'So you...you *do* remember?'

Casimiro gave a little click of disapproval as he pulled his speech from his jacket pocket and prepared to wave her away.

'Do you realise how many people I "meet" in the course of my working life?' he demanded impatiently. 'And while they will each remember every detail of our encounter, most of their faces are, to me, simply a blur. What was it? Some official line-up you were on? Some catering college I was visiting?'

'No. You don't understand.' Shaking her head, Melissa could see the look of surprise in his eyes as she contradicted him, but she was fearless now. This was her last chance, she realised. Her very last chance.

'What don't I understand?' he asked, dangerously.

'This was different.'

Casimiro tensed, half wondering if she was one of that thankfully rare breed of women who stalked famous men—and whether he had been foolish in granting her access. But something in the way she was looking at him made his eyes narrow and his heart began to pound. He glanced over to where Orso was clearly poised to terminate the conversation at his behest. At the guards who stood in the shadows and could be summoned at a moment's notice. 'Go on.'

Melissa was aware that he was in full view of everyone in the banquet hall. And that there seemed something terribly wrong about disclosing something as big as this before the curious gaze of an international audience. 'If you don't mind, I'd rather go somewhere…a little more private.'

'I don't think so,' he said softly. 'You've already had more than enough concessions. You've got your opportunity—which is precisely two minutes—to tell me what all this damned mystery is about.' His mouth hardened. 'And it had better be good.'

Her voice was trembling but somehow she got the words out. 'Our meeting was very different from most you must encounter, Your Majesty—or, at least, I'm assuming it was. It was back in the summer nearly two years ago—in England—at a party during a tour of the Zaffirinthos marbles. In fact, we did more than meet. Much more. As it happens, we had a short affair and, as a consequence…' She saw the disbelief and the anger which was beginning to blaze from his amber eyes

'…as a consequence, I…I have a little son. Or, rather, *we* have a son. What I should say is…you have a son, Your Majesty.'

CHAPTER THREE

CASIMIRO stared into Melissa's white face, his heart beginning to pound with fury at her outrageous claim. *He*, a father of *her* child? He would have liked to have taken her by her shoulders and to have shaken the admission from her that her words were nothing but a sham and a lie.

But he knew that all eyes were upon him, just as they always were, for hadn't he spent a lifetime being watched—like the human equivalent of a goldfish? Wasn't he always seated at the top table or the raised dais for precisely that purpose? Kings were not permitted the freedom to express their feelings and therefore he could not indulge in the luxury of venting his anger towards this insolent Englishwoman. The only outward sign of his ire was the clenching of his fists beneath the table—and so great was his wrath that he barely noticed that he had crushed the heavy cream parchment of his abdication speech in the process.

He leaned towards her by a fraction—as if he were about to engage in some pleasantry about the food. 'Are you crazy?' he said, his accusation so soft that nobody but Melissa could hear it. 'One of those crazy women who go around pretending to have been impregnated by powerful men?'

Melissa flinched—recoiling from the naked anger in his eyes. 'No! No! Of course not. I'm telling the truth.'

'And I don't believe you.'

'Why not?' she whispered, shocked by his venom.

'You want me to spell it out for you?' He wanted to hurt her now—to lash back at her for daring to concoct such a wild fantasy. To show his extreme displeasure for daring to disrupt his plans. With the hand which wasn't holding his crushed speech, he indicated the array of glitteringly beautiful women who sat at each sparkling and flower-festooned table gazing up at him with the adoration of teenagers at a boy-band concert.

'You think that I can't have any woman I want in my bed? You don't think I'm spoilt for choice by all the females who daily throw themselves at me?' His eyes became cold. 'Do the maths, *cara*,' he added icily. 'If I could have my pick of the most beautiful women in the world, then why the hell would I choose someone like you?'

Melissa swallowed, knowing there was no answer to this—because, deep down, wasn't he simply echoing her own sentiments? Hadn't she found it unbelievable at the time that such a man should have chosen to take someone like her as his lover? So she couldn't really blame him for coming out and saying it now. She had no right to feel hurt by what was essentially the truth—but one thing still didn't add up. One thing that was pretty painful to accept. 'So you don't even remember me?' she said woodenly.

At this, Casimiro felt his heart quicken and perhaps

Orso recognised his disquiet, for his aide stepped forward at just that moment.

'Majesty? Shall I conduct Miss Maguire back to the kitchens? The time for your speech approaches.'

Casimiro let his gaze flick briefly over the abdication speech which now lay crumpled in his hand. How your life could change in one brief second, he thought bitterly. He should have been about to announce a major change in direction. A new freedom. But now...

His gaze moved to the Englishwoman, staring at the determination in her green eyes, which was at odds with the trembling of her lips. He did not know if she was crazy, or if this was some kind of audacious blackmail scheme. But there was enough plucky defiance in her gaze to make him pause and something about her lilac-scented defiance which made him determined to delve a little deeper. He wondered how much she knew. Or guessed. And suddenly the certainty hit him. His plans were not ruined completely—but they must certainly be put on hold. At least until he established that she was simply a fantasist. And in the meantime—she must be given an indication that it was he who held the power. *All* the power.

'Yes, take her away,' he clipped out. 'And I shall begin.'

She tried one last time. 'Majesty—'

'Go,' he ordered. '*Go!*'

Melissa was so shocked at his angry dismissal—at the fact that he could wave her away like a troublesome insect in the light of what she'd just told him—that she found herself following Orso from the dais as if she were on autopilot.

Feeling numb, she halted when they had reached one of the far alcoves and the aide turned to her, his eyes making no attempt to hide their hostility.

'You will not attempt to contact the King again,' he said coldly. 'Ever. Do you understand?'

Part of her wanted to cry out that it was none of his business what she did, but Melissa had neither the strength nor the wherewithal to contradict him. Besides, what could she do? If she told Orso the reason for her insistence then he really *would* have her removed from the palace. If Casimiro himself didn't believe her about Ben—then it stood to reason that nobody else would. She didn't exactly fit the profile of a discarded royal mistress, did she?

Snatches of the King's speech echoed through the hall as she bent to pick up a spray of roses which had fallen from one of the giant flower displays. She heard him commend the marriage of his brother and the subsequent birth of their son. She heard his deep, accented voice say words like 'celebration' and 'new life' and they seemed to only add to her inner pain, if that were possible.

'...and so I ask you to raise your glasses to my dear brother, Xaviero, and his beautiful wife, Princess Catherine.'

Melissa glanced over at the beautiful, laughing blonde English Princess and felt a lump which felt suspiciously like envy rise in her throat.

Somehow she got through the remainder of the banquet and at midnight she begged Stephen if she could slip away—something she wouldn't normally have dreamed of until the final guest had gone home. Maybe her face was white, or maybe something in her voice alarmed

him, because he frowned and asked her if she was ill—
and then told her to go straight to bed.

'Don't forget we're leaving in the morning,' he said.

As if she could forget something like that. She would
never set foot on this island again—nor Ben grow to
know his father as she had so hoped. Nobody could say
she hadn't tried—but one day she was going to have to
have a painful conversation with her beloved son.

She walked back to the house they'd provided for
her, which stood within the grounds of the vast palace
complex, but she didn't go straight to bed. She was
so unsettled that even attempting to sleep would have
been a complete waste of time. And although there was
every state-of-the-art diversion you could think of, she
couldn't imagine summoning up any interest in a DVD
or one of the books which took up an entire wall of the
sumptuous sitting room.

She found herself missing Ben and wishing that she
could ring him. But even if it hadn't been so late—you
couldn't really speak to a thirteen-month-old baby on
the phone, could you? She'd tried it when she arrived
yesterday. According to her aunt, Ben had kept trying to
snatch the handset and hurl it to the ground—and once
he'd worked out that it was his mother at the other end
of the line he had burst into noisy howls of rage.

Instead, Melissa packed her small suitcase—layering
in her jeans and her tops and her work-clothes. Afterwards, she stripped off her clothes and took a shower—
telling herself that tomorrow night she would be standing
beneath the half-hearted splutter of tepid water in her
tiny bathroom at home and to make the most of this un-
paralleled luxury while she had the chance.

But it was hard to be enthusiastic in such circumstances and the powerful jets of water and the lavish
array of soaps and shampoos did little to distract her
swirling thoughts. Plan A had been to tell Casimiro
about Ben—and that had failed spectacularly. She didn't
even *have* a Plan B.

Towelling herself dry and raking a comb through the
dark wet strands of her hair, Melissa pulled on the over-
sized T-shirt which had been given to her by one of her
clients and which she now wore as a nightie. She'd just
finished boiling the kettle to make herself a cup of herbal
tea when there was a low but insistent knocking at the
front door, and she glanced at her watch and frowned.

Getting on for two o'clock—surely Stephen wouldn't
come calling this late?

The tapping resumed and her heart began to pound—
because unless it was the dreaded Orso about to kick
her off the complex, there was only one person Melissa
could imagine knocking this late.

Tiptoeing over to the door, she drew a deep breath.
'Who is it?'

'Who the hell do you think it is?'

He didn't sound like a king when he said that, and
when Melissa pulled open the door, he didn't much look
like a king either. In those faded denim jeans which
showcased his endlessly long legs and a black T-shirt
emphasising the muscular wall of his torso, he looked
more like some off-duty film star.

But the way he strode past her and then kicked the
door shut with an impatience he couldn't conceal was
pure royal arrogance and anger.

As he turned to face her, trying to control the ragged

rage of his breathing, Casimiro's eyes scanned her in disbelief. Her long dark hair was drying in some kind of wild cloud around her head and she was wearing an awful shapeless grey garment which carried a picture of a giant cell phone and asked the question: *Are You Turned On?*

His lips curved in distaste—but the tacky sentiment must have subliminally registered in his subconscious because he started noticing that her long legs were completely bare. And that she had no polish on her toes. And that her small breasts were pushing against the fabric of her T-shirt—their shape outlined and their tips as hard as tiny diamonds.

It was inexplicable and ridiculous that he should find such a woman attractive and yet he would have been a liar if he had denied the stab of desire which began to tug at his groin.

But he swiftly pushed that from his mind—acknowledging that her extraordinary statement had somehow managed to influence him and that he had stopped short of giving his abdication speech. How dared she? How *dared she*?

'Wh-what are you doing here?' she questioned as she met the blaze of fury which sparked from his amber eyes.

What indeed? Hadn't the faint drift of her lilac scent been as much a driving force as his need to call her bluff and establish that she was nothing but a fantasist? 'I want to know what it is you want from me,' he demanded.

'I want you to be part of your son's life.'

'No.' He shook his dark head. 'You're missing the point. You don't seem to realise that your little fantasy

is a complete waste of time. Get real, why don't you?'
Amber eyes iced into her. 'You see—you are the last
person who would ever be the mother of my child.'

She stared at him in confusion. 'What…what are you
talking about?'

'Weren't you listening earlier?' He gave a sardonic
laugh. 'I tend to climb a little higher up the social ladder
when I'm choosing lovers, *cara.*'

Don't react to his insults, she told herself fiercely.
*Because that's what he wants you to do. You need to
hang onto every shred of self-control you possess.* Because this had now transcended everything other than
her fight for her little boy and she was like an angry
tigress protecting her cub. Let him say what he liked
about *her*—but she would hold firm in her conviction.
Tilting her chin in defiance, she felt the drying strands
of her thick hair falling down her back as she met his
arrogant stare—no longer cowed by the distaste that she
met in the amber eyes.

'But other than my obvious *social unsuitability* to
cavort with a monarch—there are no other reasons?'
she questioned coolly.

'Oh, there are plenty,' he demurred silkily. 'I like my
women blonde. And curvy. You're neither. In addition,
I expect them to dress exquisitely. In fact, the kind of
woman with whom I'm *intimate* puts only the finest
silk-satin and lace lingerie next to her body.' His lips
curved in derision as they flicked over her T-shirt. 'Not
something which might be worn by someone living by
the roadside.'

Still she didn't react, even though she felt as if he were
aiming darts at her heart. Destroying all the feelings

she'd once had for him—feelings she'd allowed to grow as Ben had grown. She'd remembered his kindness to her. His tenderness when he'd held her in his arms. In her head, she had built on those memories, brick by brick. She had nurtured a fantasy man in her imagination, she realised—because the real man was nothing but an arrogant and hurtful *bastard*.

'So my hair's the wrong colour, my body's the wrong shape and I dress like a tramp.' Melissa paused and then looked at him boldly. 'Anything else you've missed?'

Casimiro frowned, because her persistence was surprising. By now she should have caved in. Started blubbing and giving him some hard-luck story about how she really needed money. She wanted financial aid for an ailing donkey sanctuary. She was battling to preserve a rare butterfly threatened by the proposed new road which would raze through its natural habitat. She was sorry to have invented such a far-fetched story but she was desperate…

'Actually, yes.' His voice was stealthy now. 'I always use protection when I make love to a woman.' He saw her cheeks grow pink. Would this graphic truth be enough to get her to back down? he wondered. 'There's a general consensus, you see—which deems that my seed is precious stuff. More precious than most.' His mouth twisted into a knowingly sarcastic smile. 'It's a King thing.'

She paused for a moment to let this outrageous comment die away. 'So why are you here?' she questioned quietly.

Again, her general unflappability when faced with his unmistakable anger slightly wrong-footed him. Why *was* he here? If he had really believed that she was some cheap con-artist then she wouldn't have got within a million miles of him. So why? Why was it that when he looked at her, he felt the faint tug of something he couldn't quite put his finger on? Something which felt unfamiliar and uncomfortable.

Since his accident—when his life had hung in the balance for days—so many of his usual pastimes had been curtailed that it felt an age since he had tasted danger. But he could taste it now. It seemed to linger in the air about him—tantalising him—just as the highest jump on one of his beloved horses had always tantalised him.

He hadn't ridden since the accident—but now came enticement in a different and unexpected form. Not blonde. Not petite, nor curvy—but bold and brunette with long, long legs and eyes which were the greenest he had ever seen. Almost emerald… Once again he felt the distant tug of something nebulous—some tantalising memory which hovered just out of reach.

He touched the tip of his tongue to his upper lip, slid it slowly over the surface. 'Maybe I came looking for something to nudge my memory,' he said softly.

She hadn't realised what he was about to do—because in Melissa's book, you didn't come onto a woman if you had just spent the last ten minutes insulting her and looking at her as if she'd crawled out from underneath a stone.

But to her shock he was pulling her into his arms with a proprietary and arrogant air. Pulling her really close—so that all that lay between her and his hard, lean torso were just two thin layers of their respective T-shirts. Suddenly, she could feel the sheer pleasure of being touched by him again and—despite the circumstances—it felt just as amazing as it had ever done. Her skin began to sing and her heart to pound, but this wasn't right. Deep down, she knew it wasn't right…

'What…what the hell do you think you're doing?' she breathed.

Her stumbled little protest both angered and inflamed him, so that another hot urgent jerk of desire pressed hard against the denim of his jeans. Pushing a strand of dark hair away from her pale face, he stared down into the pure green colour of her darkening eyes.

'Make your mind up, *cara mia*,' he bit out throatily. 'You say that I've been your lover—'

'I say it because it's *true*!'

'Then maybe the taste of your lips and the feel of your body will jog my memory. *Capisca?*'

He lowered his mouth onto hers, capturing her lips in a kiss so hard that it made her shudder for all kinds of reasons. She shuddered because, as a kiss, it felt almost contemptuous and a million miles away from any real tenderness or regard. And she shuddered because he kissed with a masterly skill which took her breath away. And, of course, because it had been so long. Much, much too long.

'*Casimiro*,' she breathed—the word itself a luxury, because surely you were permitted to call a king by name when he was kissing you?

'*Dio*—' He felt her lips open beneath his—and her instantaneous response cut through his defences—as if he had been unprepared for such immediate passion. Had he expected more of a fight? Even *wanted* more of a fight—so that he would have had to kiss her into some sort of submission and force her to retract her ridiculous claim?

But there was no fight as her rangy body melted against his—the small but perfect breasts flowering into life, her sighing delight made irresistible by the accompanying soft swivel of her hips. Casimiro felt his jutting erection positioned in perfect alignment to her and he uttered a small curse beneath his breath.

He had meant to give her a swift demonstration of his sexual power. To have her weak and wanting him—her body soft with yearning—and in this he had succeeded. But by now he should have terminated the kiss. To have thrust her away with a contemptuous remark about how any man could surely be the father of her child if she was so free and easy with her favours.

So why were his lips plundering hers with a hunger which had never felt so keen? And why were his fingers clasping one of her breasts—feeling the iron-hard little peak puckering through her T-shirt?

'Oh!' she gasped, knowing that she should stop him—but how the hell could her love-starved body stop him from doing something which was so incredible? Running her fingers distractedly through the thick tumble of his ebony hair, she felt a faint little raised line which zig-zagged from behind his ear to just beside his temple, and for a brief second she frowned. But only for a second—because the way he was touching her drove all sane thoughts from her mind. *'Casimiro,'* she breathed again, the word sounding like a prayer and an incitement.

Her easy acquiescence both thrilled and angered him—her breathless little moans spurring him until he was rucking up the baggy T-shirt like a schoolboy eager for his first intimate touch of a woman. *And she was letting him.*

He gave a groan of delight as his hand skated up and over her inner thighs and for one tantalising moment he paused, heard her hold her breath.

'You are *good*,' he ground out, tearing his lips away from hers in an attempt to suck in a ragged supply of oxygen to his lungs. Too good, he thought—as the desire to unzip himself and impale her heated his blood with a terrible kind of primitive yearning.

'So are you,' she whispered, wanting him to kiss her again. And more. Much more. Was he remembering the feel of her body and the fact that they were so good together—as she was? Would it be such a terrible thing to carry on with what they'd been doing—to show Casimiro that their son had been given life as a result of an act as amazing as this?

'I want you,' he ground out.

'And I want…I want *you*,' came her shuddered response.

Yet even as he felt the restlessness in her body which matched his own, Casimiro knew that this was crazy. Still his hand lingered on the cool thigh and the temptation to trail it towards its sweet destination almost overwhelmed him. He could have her in an instant. Here. Now. On the floor. In her bed—and then what?

'No. This is not going to happen.' Abruptly, he let his hand fall and stepped away from her—observing the disbelief and disappointment which had darkened her green eyes, the rapid rising and falling of her perfect little breasts as her fingers flew to her lips. And Casimiro could do nothing to stop the tide of relief which flooded over him—eclipsing even the aching frustration in his aroused body. For he had demonstrated to them both the power of his steely will! Of his iron-hard resolve. Let her know the kind of person she was dealing with—and then let her go on her way!

He allowed himself a brief moment of satisfaction— for he could not imagine any other man who would have turned down such a delicious, sensual feast, so willingly offered up. Seeing her begin to tug down the rumpled T-shirt over her slim thighs, he turned his back to allow her a moment to regain her composure. And he his.

When he turned back, she had raked her hands back through her mussed hair—its silken strands still drying in disarray over her narrowed shoulders. Her cheeks were very pink and she was staring at him with an expression which was a mixture of embarrassment and defiance.

'You are very free with your favours,' he observed slowly.

'As are you with yours!' she returned. 'Tell me, is *that* why you can't remember me—because you've had so many women that they all blur into one?'

There was a deliberate pause as his eyes raked over her, anger spitting amber fire from his eyes. 'You dare to speak to me in such an insolent way?'

'Maybe I'm just copying you!' The words bubbled out indignantly. 'Or do you think it's a one-way street when it comes to insults? That I'm going to let you say what you like about me just because you happen to be a king and I'm just a lowly commoner? Especially when we both know what you're really doing is shying away from your responsibilities.'

'*Shying away from my responsibilities?*' he echoed incredulously.

'Well, aren't you? All I'm asking is that you see Ben. Just once. Just see him and realise that he's yours. What have you got to lose?'

Casimiro stared at her and gave a grim kind of smile. More than she would ever know. Much, much more. If he had an heir, then everything would change. His life and his future would alter in the most dramatic fashion.

But as he stared at her he knew that she wasn't going to go away easily—and that if he let her it would leave a million questions unanswered. Questions which might come back to haunt him and would leave him unable to make his abdication with an easy heart.

'And what if I do see him,' he questioned slowly, 'and still do not believe that he is mine—then will you agree to give up this cause of yours? Give up and go away— leave me alone for ever?'

This stark demand pained her far more than it should have done because it was an indication of just how much he wanted her gone from his life. But of course he did— he'd never wanted her in any way but as a quick fling, had he? If it had been just about her then she would have walked away right then, with her head held high—but it wasn't just about her. And what choice did she have? Melissa knew that she was going to have to agree to his hurtful clause if ever she was going to have some sense of closure. It was a gamble, yes—but a gamble she had to take. For Ben's sake.

Staring into the hard, golden gleam of his amber eyes, she opened her mouth to agree to his terms when something began to trouble her. Something which didn't make sense.

Why was he agreeing to see Ben if he was so certain that the child couldn't be his? And why *couldn't* he remember her? Melissa knew that she wasn't the kind of woman who turned heads, but this hadn't been some forgettable one-night stand they'd shared. It had been the best part of five days *and she had been a virgin*. And deep down she didn't really believe that he'd had so many partners that he couldn't distinguish one from the other.

His face was shadowed and sombre. She looked at his thick dark hair—all ruffled where she'd been frantically running her fingers through it. At the faint scar at his temple which now lay revealed. The slightly raised little zigzagging line she had discovered when he'd been kissing her. She knew every inch of the man by heart—for hadn't she touched him lovingly and eagerly as often as she could when they'd been lovers? And one thing was for sure—he'd never had that jagged little scar on his head back then. Which meant that it must have been a legacy from his fall.

Suddenly it all made sense. Complete and believable sense. It was so simple that she couldn't believe why she hadn't thought about it before.

'That's why you don't remember me,' she said suddenly.

Casimiro stilled. 'What the hell are you talking about?'

'When you had your accident,' she said slowly. 'The one that nearly killed you. The one which meant your brother had to act as Prince Regent while you lay stricken.'

'That's history,' he snapped—because the dawning look of comprehension on her face was making him uneasy. 'Which I don't particularly want to rake up.'

'Maybe it is—but the past always impacts on the present, doesn't it? You don't remember me because you can't. The knock on your head must have wiped the memory clean away.' She drew a deep breath and looked at him with eyes which were suddenly soft with understanding. 'You're suffering from amnesia and that's why I mean nothing to you, isn't it, Casimiro?'

CHAPTER FOUR

CASIMIRO felt a brutal kind of rage wash over him as he stared at Melissa. At her passion-flushed cheeks and the way her eyes looked almost emerald as she levelled her accusation at him.

You're suffering from amnesia and that's why I mean nothing to you.

His hands clenched into fists by the tensed shafts of his thighs as fury fizzed through his veins. Because nobody but her had guessed that a brief segment of time had been shaved from his memory. Nobody. So how could such a woman as this see through to the truth where all others had failed?

'How the hell do you work that out?' he demanded icily.

She noticed that he hadn't denied it. Her eyes drifted to his temple, and despite his harshness towards her, she found herself biting her lip as she imagined him lying there, hurt. 'When I saw that little…scar.'

Casimiro's mouth hardened as he heard the emotional break in her voice—wondering if it was spontaneous or contrived. 'You are cleverer than I imagined,' he said. And probably just as manipulative, he reminded himself grimly. How delighted she would be to discover that she knew more about him than his courtiers or even his brother! And yet, in some crazy way—wasn't it something of a relief to be able to share the burden of his amnesia with someone?

'So you're not denying that Ben could be your son?' she questioned hopefully.

Ben. Casimiro frowned. Giving the child a name only added another layer of complexity to the affair.

'I am conceding that it is a possibility.'

It was better than nothing and Melissa bit her lip, wanting to blurt out her gratitude and yet some instinct stopping her from doing anything more than silently nodding her head.

Casimiro studied her. He had been about to leave— to slam his way out and to make arrangements about a trip to England to see the child at some undetermined point in the future—while still nurturing the hope that she was a complete fantasist. But her perception had changed everything.

He felt a pulse beat at his temple—because what she had learned was dangerous. Would she try to use the knowledge she'd gained to secure a place for herself in his life? he wondered. Knowledge was power—everyone knew that—and maybe it was time for a little redistribution of that power. Why waste his energy on pointless rage, when there was a much more satisfactory outlet which would serve him better...?

Slowly, he let his gaze drift over her. At the fall of dark shiny hair which was now completely dry and shimmering around her narrow shoulders. At the bare legs and the unvarnished toenails. Beneath that hideous garment, she was completely naked; he knew that for himself. And once again—despite his avowal of her un-suitability—he felt the hot, hard shimmering of desire.

'Come over here,' he said silkily.

Melissa blinked. She had been expecting anger—especially when she'd seen the shadowed expression on his face. But his face wasn't looking in the least bit threatening now. On the contrary. She narrowed her eyes, wondering if she was misreading it. Seeing something there that she wanted to see rather than what really was.

But no.

His expression looked…inviting. Vital. The lips had softened—as if they were illustrating just how kissable they really were. And his eyes were dark—really dark—with that opaque kind of blackness which even someone with Melissa's scant experience knew meant that he wanted her.

'Why?' she whispered, her heart beginning to pound.

'Don't let's play games—not now. You know exactly why.'

'But you just, just—'

'Pushed you away?'

'*Yes.*'

'Maybe I've realised what a fool I was being. Or maybe I just needed time for my body to make its protest known. And it is—believe me, it is—very loud and very clear.' Glancing down with a rueful expression, he shrugged. 'So come over here, Melissa.'

'No,' she said, in a small voice.

'No? You refuse your King?'

'You are not *my* King and, yes, I am refusing you.'

'Why?'

'Because…' *Because you've already made a fool of*

me. Because you could break my heart into a million pieces. 'Because I'm here to discuss my son—and it's not appropriate.'

'Not *appropriate*?' he mocked.

'N-no.'

'You think there's some kind of social guideline for the bizarre situation in which we find ourselves?' he demanded, but, interestingly, her words only inflamed his growing desire—because refusal was something which Casimiro never encountered. 'Then it seems that I must come to you, *bella mia*.'

Her eyes widened in alarm but she could do nothing about the sudden prickle of her senses as he began to walk towards her with the determination and the stealth of a predator which had just spotted a particularly accessible morsel lying waiting for him.

'Don't,' she whispered.

'Don't what? At least *try* to say it as if you mean it,' he drawled, his mouth hardening into a smile as he reached for her and pulled her into his arms.

It wasn't his touch—but the smile which sealed it. This one was hard and somehow grim, but it was a smile all the same and it catapulted her back to bittersweet time when she'd seen a much softer variation. When desire had ruled their lives and there had been no shame in it.

'But why this…*frown*?' Casimiro's voice had deepened as he smoothed the small crease in her brow, tracing his fingertip down to outline the sudden trembling of her lips.

'Can't you guess?' she whispered.

He read the wariness in her eyes and recognised that she was going to have to be cajoled into submission. That she was cleverer and feistier than he'd given her credit for—and that if he wanted her co-operation, then he was going to have to seduce her. *Really* seduce her. For there was no surer way of getting a woman to consent to a man's agenda than by making her a prisoner of her own senses.

Because he needed Melissa Maguire, he realised. Needed her to remind him of the missing fragment of his past and to see what lay in it.

He felt the slow simmer of anticipation as he gazed down at the trembling of her lips.

And she needed him, too. Much, much more.

Again, he traced the outline of her lips with his fingertip, seeing her eyes cloud as she looked up at him. 'You don't like me doing this?' he questioned silkily. 'And yet minutes ago you were writhing around in my arms—your body silently begging me to take you.'

Melissa swallowed, for the fingertip was now stroking its way along her jaw. It was an almost innocuous touch and yet it had activated an aching kind of hunger which made every nerve ending instantly feel as if it were on fire.

'I know. But that's not what we're here for, Casimiro. We're supposed to be…to be…' She wanted to tell him that they needed to talk some more. About Ben. About what was going to happen now. But how could she manage to utter a single word of objection when his lips were now on her neck?

'Shh.' He felt her head tip back—like a flower which was too heavy for its stem—giving him access to the smooth expanse of skin.

'We should…should…' She wanted to say that they

should stop it because that was what she knew she *ought* to say. Some inner voice of caution telling her that it was a mistake to let him take her as easily as this. But her love-starved body and her idealistic heart had craved this moment too much to be able to resist it and her words drifted away like bubbles as his hand reached down to cup her breast. His thumb began roughly teasing a nipple to acutely sensitive life—and Melissa felt the quick flood of blood to her veins as her body responded to him.

'*Sí, cara*—I know we should. And what is more, we're going to. Right now—just like we both want to.' The declaration was honeyed, irresistible and undeniable as Casimiro began to ruck up the baggy T-shirt—his hand alighting on the flesh of her inner thigh to where a woman was always soft. But Melissa's skin was like cool silk, he thought—a tantalising contrast to the molten heat which was beckoning him inexorably upwards.

It had been so long, he realised with a jolt. Like an empty arid waste of time since he had last made love to a woman. His heart had not been in it and neither had his body—but now the hunger and the need had returned like an urgent fire which was consuming him. For one fleeting moment, he questioned his sanity, it having chosen *this* woman with whom to break his self-imposed curfew. Until he caught the unmistakable scent of her arousal in the air and again felt her restlessness as his fingers trickled enticing little circles over her thigh.

For a moment he tantalised her. Letting his hand linger there—inches away from its sweet destination. Hearing her sharp intake of breath as she waited to see if he would continue. He left it just long enough to make her frantic. To make her flesh crave his touch. And to hear her stumbled little gasp of relief as he plunged his fingers into her molten warmth.

'*Oh!*'

'Oh, but you wanted that, didn't you?'

'Yes, *yes*!'

'Wanted it badly?'

'*Yes!*'

'How badly?'

She knew what he was doing. Playing power games with her even while his fingers were inflicting such sweet torture. She knew that a stronger woman might have torn herself away. Looked at him with a cold dignity and told him that she would not negotiate anything which revolved around sex.

But Melissa wasn't feeling strong right then. She felt helpless and torn by conflicting emotions as he lowered his lips to her ear.

'This badly?' he questioned as he began to move his fingers intimately against her aroused flesh.

She closed her eyes. *Tell him no.* Tell him no. But her fists, which had been tightly clenched by her side now unfurled themselves, like daisies in the heat of the sun. 'Yes. *Yes.* Oh, please—yes!'

He could feel her pleasure building quickly, inexorably, and in normal circumstances he might have brought her swiftly to orgasm before seeking his own fulfilment. But these were not normal circumstances. Urgently, he looked around. The floor? Or the bed? His mouth hardened. No, definitely not the bed. Take her to bed and he might just be tempted to spend the night with her.

Without warning he picked her up and carried her

over to one of the sofas, slowing sliding her to her feet and then tilting her chin up so that she was caught in the cross-fire of his amber eyes. 'Now undress me,' he commanded unsteadily.

Melissa wasn't exactly a novice, but that was what it felt like—until she reminded herself that Casimiro had taught her everything she knew. Her fingers were trembling, but somehow she managed to free the button and then the zip of his jeans. Gently jerking it down over the massively aroused shaft, she heard him give a strangled little groan of pleasure.

She felt shy almost as the formidable power of him sprang free—almost too shy to touch him—and was glad when, impatiently, he pushed her hand away to yank off his jeans. He pulled the T-shirt over his head, and with a single scoop peeled off her own baggy nightwear, his eyes scanning her body only briefly—as if he was not content with visual stimulation. As if he couldn't wait...

But he waited long enough to pull a silver-foil packet from the pocket of his discarded jeans and Melissa flinched as she stared at it.

'Were you so sure I'd agree to make love with you, Casimiro?'

'Was I so very wrong, then?' he mocked.

'Or do you always come prepared?' she whispered as he pushed her down onto the soft cushions of the sofa.

'You are in no position to interrogate me,' he murmured, his lips against her ear as he placed his hands on either side of her narrow hips and lowered himself down on her. 'In fact, you are in a position to do one thing and one thing only, *mia bella*. And that is this...*this*!'

With an urgent groan, he thrust deep into her body and Melissa gasped with pleasure, clinging to his shoulders as he moved inside her—so hot and so hard that it took her breath away. She could feel the heat building—spiralling out of all control—barely able to believe it was happening so quickly. She hardly had a moment to reacquaint herself with the sweet pleasures of sex, when suddenly the world began to splinter and shatter around her and she cried out in an orgasm that had her vulnerable and helpless and trembling in his arms.

Dimly, she was aware of his own drawn-out moan of completion, and the way his muscular body shuddered inside her as she struggled to hold onto her composure—a strong cocktail of painful feelings threatening to override the warm satiation of her body. And unable to prevent the slow slide of tears down her cheeks as she contemplated what she had just done.

Reality returning with the slowing beats of his heart, Casimiro bent his head and kissed her—his face drawing back a little as he tasted salt on her lips. With a frown, he stared down into her brimming eyes as some rogue thought came drifting into his mind from nowhere. *Emerald stars*, he thought. But it was gone again in an instant.

'Tears?' he murmured as he wiped one away with the tip of his finger. But he could not wipe the smile of satisfaction from his lips. He had her exactly where he wanted her—all warm and soft and sated beneath him. She was greedy for him—and that sexual weakness would allow *him* to call all the shots. 'And here was me thinking that sexual pleasure was supposed to make you smile.'

Sexual pleasure? Melissa could have hit him. But how

could you hit a man when you were still joined intimately with him—his body still quietly pulsating inside your own? When she'd made herself so vulnerable in front of him that she felt as if he'd torn off a whole layer of skin and exposed her raw heart to the world? And she suspected that any hand she raised to strike him might instead be distracted by the lean musculature of his torso. So that she might be tempted instead to curl her fingers into the whorls of dark hair which arrowed down his chest so enticingly.

Melissa stared up at the shifting shadows of his aristocratic face.

'Now what?' she questioned unsteadily.

CHAPTER FIVE

'BEN, Ben…' Too late, Melissa reached for the pot of organic raspberry yoghurt her son was waving in the air—just in time to see it spill in a pink and lumpy cascade onto his dark curls. 'Oh, *Ben!*' she cried in horror.

'Den!' came his ecstatic response, because he hadn't yet got to grips with the letter B, and he fixed his mother with a gappy, happy grin.

Melissa plucked him out of his high chair and sent an agonised glance at the clock which was ticking on the wall. Only fifteen minutes before Casimiro was due to get here and the little boy she'd dressed so carefully was covered in gunge and smelling like a fruit sundae. His woefully inadequate bib was now sodden and she rued her decision to feed him this close to the King's arrival—but she hadn't bargained on him deciding that he was hungry and deciding that he was going to have a screaming paddy if he didn't have some pudding.

And if you hadn't been gazing at yourself in the mirror—you might have realised that he was about to dress himself in yoghurt.

Trying to calm the worryingly baleful expression in his wide amber eyes, she began to remove the ruined clothing. She'd been having a last minute look at herself only because she'd been so busy—frantically trying to make Ben look like the best-dressed and most well-adjusted baby in the world. So that she'd barely had time to do anything about her own appearance. And realising too late that she looked awful. Just the way she always seemed to look awful when Casimiro was around.

But this wasn't supposed to be about her!

She stripped Ben off and gave him a rapid bath in a few inches of tepid and soapy water before putting his nappy back on—but by now he had begun to grow furious.

'Shh, darling. Shh,' she soothed as he jerked his head away from his second-best T-shirt. But all her pacifying was to no avail and she was soon engaged in a classic mother and baby battle. Normally, she would have given in gracefully—deciding that it wasn't worth falling out over a different taste in clothes.

The sound of the doorbell stopped her in her tracks and Melissa felt that uncomfortable mixture of excitement and dread begin to grow. Casimiro. When he had telephoned and told her that he was flying to England, she hadn't really believed it. Hadn't dared believe it in case it hadn't happened. For hadn't there been a part of her which had wondered if he might just try consigning her to oblivion? Waiting to see what she would do next.

Well, it seemed that he was true to his word because he was here. Casimiro was *here*!

'This is very important, darling Ben,' she whispered as she scooped the baby up in her arms. 'There's a very important man at the door.' *He's your* Daddy, she thought, her heart thundering as she went to answer it.

From his position on the grubby doorstep, Casimiro waited impatiently for Melissa to let him in—even though he wasn't exactly overjoyed at the prospect. From the moment the car had pulled up outside the poorly built apartment block—and he'd tapped impatiently on the window and asked the driver if he'd made some kind of mistake—his senses had been shaken to the core.

A letter was missing from the communal sign on the wall and there was a smashed window on the fourth floor, which someone had repaired with a piece of cardboard. Scorched brown earth stood where grass should have been and a wilting tree was the only vegetation in sight. He had seen the two bodyguards accompanying him look around in alarm but he had ignored their repeated requests to drive on.

'I need to be here,' he stated resolutely.

'But, Majesty.'

'Enough!' he clipped out. 'You will wait here in the car until I return—do you understand?'

Clearly they could tell he meant it—though it was equally clear they didn't like it. He had made sure he'd looked as incognito as possible for this visit to see the boy who Melissa claimed was his flesh and blood, but one thing was for sure—what Casimiro had seen had taken him by surprise.

During his life, he had travelled as much as his role as heir apparent allowed—and his father had seen to it that every summer he had been schooled by tutors from a variety of different countries. Of *course* he knew that he was immensely privileged and wealthy—and of *course* he knew that not everyone enjoyed such a rarefied standard of living as he did. But he had never known anyone on a personal level who actually *lived* like this.

It didn't get any better. The stone stairwell leading to Melissa's flat was dark and dank and the paint on her front door was peeling. His mouth curved as he uttered a silent prayer that the whole thing had been some kind of terrible error. That in the fortnight since she'd left Zaffirinthos she'd discovered the identity of the *real* father. And it wasn't him. Some postman perhaps. Or a man who worked in the local garage. Anyone but him.

Jamming his thumb on the doorbell, he was forced to wait what seemed like an age until Melissa appeared at the door holding a squirming baby who seemed only half dressed.

'I'm s-so sorry,' she stumbled. 'Ben's had a bit of an accident.'

'An *accident*?' he bit out, feeling an instinctive chill of alarm.

'Oh, nothing serious. He's just tipped yoghurt over himself and is furious because he had to have an emergency bath and now he's refusing to let me dress him.'

Casimiro frowned. He was no stranger to babies—for didn't Xaviero and Catherine have the infant Cosimo, whom he saw from time to time? But Cosimo was always drafted in on high days and holidays—looking immaculate in crisp white romper suits embroidered with blue silken rabbits or little yellow aeroplanes. Once he had seen his nephew after his bathtime but he looked nothing like this angry little creature—with his red cheeks and mop of dark curls. And the idea that he could possibly be the father of this little boy became more far-fetched by the minute.

'May I come in?' he questioned curtly.

'Yes, yes—of course. Do—please—come in.' She hated herself for caring—but naturally she cared how Casimiro saw her little home. Yes, it was humble and, no, she had neither the time nor the funds to attempt an extensive and expensive redecoration of a place she didn't want to be living in for much longer. But she had done her best with what she'd got—and for that she was grateful to the artistic eye that her boss was always raving on about.

There were bunches of cheap flowering pot-plants from the market crammed into funky little containers, a pot of coffee bubbling away and everything was as clean and as tidy as it had ever been…except for the spilt yoghurt on the high chair, of course.

Casimiro stepped over the threshold and his towering height and general air of powerful male dominance were enough to make Ben look at his mother in alarm and then open his mouth and begin to howl.

'Shh, Ben—it's all right. The man won't hurt you. Shh, darling.'

Perplexed, Casimiro stared at the bawling baby whose eyes were tightly squeezed shut and who seemed to be building up to a crescendo of tears while Melissa just stood there, chewing at her lips and looking completely powerless to stop him. He didn't know what made him do it but suddenly he expelled a low but surprisingly piercing whistle—the kind he had used to summon his beloved horse before he'd had the damned accident.

Suddenly, the child quietened. Opened his tear-filled eyes with a mixture of surprise and alarm and stared straight into Casimiro's face.

And Casimiro found himself looking into amber eyes a shade lighter than his own.

A shiver travelled up the entire length of his spine. A tiptoeing of some emotion he couldn't have described with any word from his extensive and multilingual vocabulary. Perhaps shock was there. Yes, definitely shock. And recognition, too. For Casimiro might have been described by his enemies as stubborn and arrogant—but he was not a fool. And instantly he recognised the amber eye colour which had run through his aristocratic family tree since his ancestors had first settled on the idyllic Mediterranean island of Zaffirinthos.

Melissa found herself regarding the profile of the man who dominated her small sitting room while unable to stop a sense of hope from fizzing through her veins as she saw his body suddenly tense.

'What...what do you think?' she questioned anxiously.

Casimiro turned to her. And as the possible consequences of his discovery began to dawn on him his sense of bitter frustration increased. Could this...this sturdy little scrap of humanity really be his? And yet, given the evidence of his eyes—could he belong to anyone *but* him? He saw the eagerness which had crumpled Melissa's lips and he thought that she looked like a stallholder at the end of an unprofitable market day—who sensed that they were about to make their biggest sale of all.

'Perhaps you could be a little more specific?' he said tightly.

The tone didn't *sound* hopeful—but Melissa refused

to quieten the small prayer which was running through her mind.

'About...' She didn't want to say 'your son'—not now, not when he was here. It seemed a little presumptuous, under the circumstances. 'About Ben,' she finished, with a quick, apprehensive smile.

Ignoring the unfamiliar ache in his heart as he looked down at the wet-haired baby who wore nothing but a nappy, Casimiro dealt with the question on an entirely superficial level as kings could do almost better than anyone. 'Is this how he always greets guests?'

Hiding her hurt, she drew her shoulders back defensively. 'I told you—he tipped yoghurt over himself.'

Glancing around the shabby room, he returned his gaze to her face, but his voice was filled with concern rather than censure. 'And is this any way to bring up a child who you claim is heir to my throne?'

'We haven't a lot of choice,' she said defensively—too proud to spell out in detail her precarious financial state. 'And anyway—he's happy.'

'Is he?'

Dark brows were elevated in disbelief and Melissa realised that it was a stupid thing to say under the circumstances since Ben had only just stopped crying. And looking at the scruffy room through Casimiro's privileged eyes—could she really blame him for thinking otherwise?

'Yes! Yes, of course he's happy!'

But Ben had now started squirming and rubbing his fist into each eye in the way he always did when he was tired. And even though she longed to put him down in his cot—some sense of foreboding made her want to keep him up for as long as possible.

To act as a buffer between her and Casimiro? she wondered guiltily.

Ben gave another wriggle and Melissa sighed as she gave into the inevitable. 'I'll have to go and put him to bed.' She hesitated as she was overwhelmed by a terrible and slightly hysterical urge to ask him in a sing-song voice if he wanted 'to say goodnight to Daddy'? But common sense prevailed and she turned on her heel and went to get her son ready for bed, aware that Casimiro didn't follow her. So there was to be no touching fairy-tale scene where the King's hard heart melted over a bedtime story.

Somehow, she carried on with her usual routine. She wound up the brightly coloured plastic mobile above his bed which played 'Baa Baa Black Sheep' and she joined in with the nursery rhyme the way she always did. Smoothing her fingers through the silken tumble of his curls, she ran a gentle and loving palm down the side of his peachy-soft skin.

'Goodnight, darling Ben,' she whispered as she turned on the night light.

She had taken so long to settle him that, when she returned to the sitting room, Melissa half hoped that Casimiro might have grown bored with waiting and gone away—knowing that such a hope was foolish and irra-tional considering all the trouble she'd gone to in order to get him here. But, no, he was still there—a captive if unwilling audience—and it was up to her to make him realise that she was telling the truth.

It had been a fortnight since she'd seen him—when

she'd stupidly let him seduce her on his island of Zaffirinthos. He had left her lying naked and confused on the sofa—his back turned to her as he had dressed in stony silence—and then suddenly agreed to travel to England to meet Ben for himself.

In those two weeks she had thought about him—actually, she'd thought about little else. Not just as a prospective father, but as a lover. He had been…what? Melissa bit her lip. He had been technically perfect yet emotionally cold during that swift coupling. Like a block of ice. Almost as if he'd enjoyed the power of bringing her to orgasm so quickly. Watching her shudder and gasp with an arrogant and triumphant look on his mockingly handsome face. And then distancing himself afterwards as if he couldn't wait to get away from her.

Well, she wasn't going to be such easy prey today—that was for sure.

'Can I offer you coffee?' she questioned politely.

'I haven't come here to endure pointless social niceties.'

'So I'll take that as a no?'

His eyes narrowed, for he did not like that hint of sarcasm in her soft English voice. He did not like it one bit. 'I have come here to discuss your extraordinary claim.'

For a moment there was silence and Melissa knew that she could dance to his particular tune all evening. Both skirting around the inevitable with nothing being achieved except more and more layers of confusion. She looked into his amber eyes, knowing that she should probably feel cowed by his mighty presence in her humble home. Or slightly ashamed at the ease with which she had let him seduce her for a second time. But in truth she felt neither. Motherhood took as much from a woman as it gave—but what it infused you with more than anything was the urgent need to fight for what was your child's right.

'Except that it's not so extraordinary now that you've seen him, is it?' she questioned quietly.

Her cool challenge took him slightly off guard. 'Meaning *what*, precisely?'

'You can't deny the eyes.'

'The eyes?'

He's deliberately misunderstanding me, thought Melissa despairingly. 'I've never seen eyes that colour on anyone else but you.'

He gave a short and bitter laugh. 'You might have trouble standing that up as a valid argument in a court of law!'

'C-court of law?'

Sensing her sudden uncertainty, he struck. 'Of course. You must surely have thought through the fact that this is not an ordinary paternity claim?'

'I don't…I don't understand.'

'Don't you?' Casimiro saw her bewilderment and felt a rush of triumph. Let her have something else to fill her head with other than thoughts of his memory loss! 'Did you really imagine that you could approach a *king*…' he paused, deliberately '…and announce that you had given birth to his son—and that he and all his people would rejoice at the news?'

'I thought…I thought…'

'What did you think, Melissa?'

'That you might be—'

'What?' he demanded. 'Pleased? Delighted? The proud papa eager to introduce his offspring to the world?'

His cruel comments deflated her growing sense of defiance, but her mother-love could see nothing but joy in her little boy. 'I thought that you would be pleased, yes—once the initial confusion had died down.'

'Initial *confusion*?' he echoed furiously. 'Are you out of your mind? Do you have *any idea* what this is going to mean?'

She stared at him, remembering his initial assessment of his son. *Is this how he always greets guests?* How callous was that as a reaction—when confronted for the first time by the delicious little scrap which was Ben? And suddenly, Melissa thought that maybe no father was better than *this* father—because what child deserved a man who seemed incapable of any kind of real feeling?

'It needn't mean anything at all,' she said fiercely. 'You're not happy about the news—fine! I've done my duty and told you—but we don't need you, Casimiro. We've managed without you up until now and we can manage without you again. Your wish is about to come true. You can go away from here now and forget about what I've told you and we will never bother you again.'

A grim smile hardened his mouth. He waited—because she was playing the inevitable game of the successful negotiator: the long, long pause before naming terms. 'So how much?' he questioned softly.

'How much?'

'Do you want me to pay you?'

There was a moment when she really didn't understand what he was talking about. When he might as well have been speaking in Greek. Until she saw the cynical golden gleam from his eyes and then she cottoned on, her heart lurching in her chest.

'You think I'm *blackmailing* you?'

'That's a rather dramatic way of putting it, Melissa. I think that "buying your silence" is the generally more acceptable term in these circumstances.'

Acceptable? *Acceptable?* Melissa found herself remembering the old childhood rhyme: *Sticks and stones can break your bones but words can never hurt you.* Who were they kidding? Words like the ones Casimiro was firing at her felt like poisoned arrows firing straight into her heart. 'You think that I want money from you?'

'Well, don't you?' he questioned coolly, his gaze flicking around the room in a disparaging assessment. 'I think that if I were in your position, I would.'

Suddenly Melissa saw her home through his eyes. The tired furniture, which no amount of bright cushions could disguise. The too-low ceilings and the windows which had obviously been low-budget when they'd been put there—but which now badly needed replacing. It was cheap. Everything in the place was on the cheap—which was why she was living here. But what would this cold-hearted beast of a man know about poverty?

'I don't want your money!' she said proudly. 'I don't want anything from you!'

'Well, we both know *that's* a lie,' he drawled.

The amber eyes gleamed at her in provocative taunt and Melissa felt colour flaring in her cheeks. How base of him to allude to that frantic coupling back on

Zaffirinthos—when she'd welcomed him into her body even though he clearly despised her and all she stood for.

'Will you please go, Casimiro?'

'But we haven't made any decisions yet.'

'There are no decisions to be made. You obviously don't want to know your son and I don't want your money. End of story.'

'Oh, but that is where you are wrong, *cara mia*.' Without warning, his hand snaked out and caught her—pulling her into the hard, muscular length of his body.

'Casimiro!' she gasped.

'The story, you see, is only just beginning,' he continued resolutely, as if she hadn't spoken.

'Wh-what are you talking about?'

'You think that you just drop a bombshell like that and then walk away from the devastation you've wreaked?'

'Devastation?'

'*Sí.*' Leaning forward, he caught the tantalising drift of lilac mixed in with soap, and yoghurt—and he felt the lustful jerk of his body in response to this strange cocktail of scents. 'If the boy—'

'Ben.'

'Ben,' he agreed reluctantly—because a sudden image of that angry little face swam uncomfortably into his mind. 'If he *is* mine—then it is going to have all kinds of repercussions on his future.' *And on mine*, he thought grimly.

'What kind of repercussions?'

His mind clearing, he looked down at her, at the wide-spaced eyes which today looked so incredibly green—possibly because the light in her apartment was so dim. At the trembling lips and the skin which looked markedly translucent because she'd tied her hair back in a ponytail. She was tall for a woman and she wore jeans which emphasised those long, long legs—and suddenly he remembered them wrapped around his naked back. Remembered her little gasps of pleasure as he thrust into her. And his own delicious completion which had followed.

'What kind?' she repeated.

Her eyes looked suddenly very bright and the soft lower cushion of her lips made him want to sink right into them. Surely there could be some *pleasurable* outcomes which could come out of this unholy mess. 'This kind,' he ground out as he lowered his mouth down onto hers.

There were all kinds of kisses, Melissa realised as she felt that first warm brush of flesh. There were tentative first kisses and those deep kisses you drowned in during sex. And then there was this kind of kiss...

It did everything a kiss was supposed to do. It made her open her lips beneath his and her knees grow weak. It made her body begin to melt against his with a terrible pent-up longing. And yet its cold execution drove home with stark emphasis just how little he respected her as a person. Devoid of any affection or regard, the seeking skill of his lips made her feel worthless—as if he had taken a hammer and whittled away at her already low self-esteem.

And she couldn't afford to let him do that!

It took every shred of resolve she had, but somehow

Melissa tore her mouth away from his—even though her traitorous body screamed out its fury.

'No!' she exclaimed—moving away from his dangerous proximity, over to the other side of the small room. Crossing her arms over her breasts as if to hide from him their prickling response, she tried to control the erratic gasping of her breath.

'No?' he echoed incredulously.

'Wh-what d-did you think was going to h-happen?' she demanded breathlessly. 'That I'd just let you walk in here and have sex with me?'

'Isn't that exactly what happened last time?' he questioned insultingly. 'You didn't exactly put up a fight.'

'And, of course, you can't remember the time before that, can you?' she said bitterly.

Casimiro's expression didn't alter. 'Remind me—did I have to woo you with wine and roses before you'd succumb? Was it a long, hard battle to get you into my bed?' he mocked, and the hot colour which flooded into her cheeks gave him, not only his answer—but also the upper hand.

Melissa bit her lip. What a cold-hearted brute he was. 'Well, nothing's going to happen this time. Apart from anything else—my son is asleep in the room next door!'

And in spite of his frustration Casimiro found her maternal prudishness oddly reassuring—since it suggested that she did not entertain a long line of lovers. 'You will need to take a DNA test,' he said suddenly.

Melissa blinked. 'I beg your pardon?'

'You heard.'

'Well, I'm not—'

'Yes,' he cut through her protest with an imperious raise of his hand. 'Yes, you are, Melissa—you have to. There is no alternative. That is, if the child is to be acknowledged as my heir.'

'But you've *seen him*!' Melissa proclaimed. 'You've seen how much he resembles you. My aunt says she's never seen eyes that colour before.'

Casimiro couldn't dispute the rarity of the shade nor its almost exclusive confinement to the ruling family of Zaffirinthos, but she was failing to see what for him was simply a fact of life.

'Do you realise how many crazies we have to deal with every year?' he questioned.

Melissa froze. 'Crazies?'

'It's one of the drawbacks of the job, Melissa—it brings all kinds of people from out of the woodwork. Futurologists who want to warn me about an imminent death threat. Men who say they knew me when we were children. Women claiming...'

'Women claiming that you've fathered their baby,' guessed Melissa slowly and she lifted pained eyes to his face. 'Is that what you think of me, then, Casimiro—that I'm some sort of "crazy"?'

For some reason her dignified little question made him feel a pang of misgiving—but he was not in a position to allow himself to listen to it. 'No, actually I don't,' he said simply. 'And none of this is about my thoughts or feelings, Melissa. It is about dealing with this matter to the best of my ability—and working out how best to present it to my people. I've examined my diary and the dates you indicated,' he continued. 'And you say the child is, how old?'

'Thirteen months,' she said dully.

He nodded. 'Yes, the times tally. I was indeed in England during the period you've indicated.'

'So if the times tally and he has the same rare eyes— then why must I have a DNA test?' she whispered.

'Because I am a *king* who is ruled by the constitution of my land,' he said, and his words had a sudden bitter resonance. 'And I do not have the freedoms which most men take for granted.'

It was an oddly brutal assessment of life at the top. Instead of all the riches and glory which came with his kingdom, Melissa suddenly caught a glimpse of an arid and rule-bound personal landscape and a feeling of fore-boding began to feather her skin. Just what can of worms was she opening up for her beloved son?

'Oh,' she said quietly. 'I see.'

He thought of his abdication speech and looked at her with renewed bitterness. 'I cannot ask my people to accept a commoner's word on a matter of such significance. Proof of paternity must be provided and a DNA test must and *will* be done. I have consulted with my advisors and they tell me there is no way round it.'

Melissa trembled at the sudden hard timbre of his words and the steely glint of resolution in his eyes. Hadn't she wished above all else for Casimiro to acknowledge his son—and didn't it seem as if that was exactly what he was about to do? Except that now she was going to have to go through the indignity of having to prove it.

Her future and Ben's determined in some anonymous laboratory.

She bit her lip. What else was it that people sometimes said? Only unlike the playground taunt of sticks and stones breaking bones—this one was true.

Oh, yes…

Be careful what you wish for—because it may just come true.

CHAPTER SIX

THE restaurant was discreet. Well, of course it was. When kings dined with commoners they didn't want the world's paparazzi jostling around outside, ready to capture the moment in all its unbelievable glory, did they?

'We need to talk,' Casimiro had announced tersely, when he'd rung her earlier that day to announce that he had the DNA results.

In a panic, Melissa had arranged for her aunt Mary to babysit—having fielded a lot of awkward questions about where she was going at such short notice. No, she wasn't working and, no, it definitely wasn't a date. She had seen her aunt's face fall—for she loved her niece and was always telling her to find herself a 'nice young man' to take care of her and Ben.

As the limousine which Casimiro had provided drew up outside the softly lit restaurant Melissa wondered what her aunt Mary would say if she knew who she was really dining with. It might have been funny if it weren't so serious—because 'nice young man' would be the last way you'd ever describe Casimiro.

The interior of the restaurant was like places she and Stephen had worked in countless times over the years—with the kind of no-cost-counted luxury which always managed to look so restrained. But this time she was here as a guest and it felt different—even if her mind hadn't been racing with apprehension about the evening ahead. Melissa's hands were clammy as she was shown to what looked like a cordoned-off section, where she could see Casimiro already seated at the table, with his back to her.

Did she imagine the expression of faint surprise on the face of the maître d' as she gave her name? Did she look so out of place in such a luxurious setting, then, or was it simply that she was in a completely different league from the other guests?

She'd done her best to cobble together an outfit which wouldn't make her stand out like a sore thumb—which shouldn't have been too difficult since Casimiro had explicitly told her to dress as if they were having a business meeting. Which in a way they were—the business of their son's future. She knew that.

So why had that simple request made her hackles rise? Was it because she felt as if he was very possibly *ashamed* of her? As if he wanted to send out the subliminal message to anyone who happened to see them eating together that she was the kind of woman who helped arrange parties but certainly not the kind of woman he ever associated with on a personal level.

Well, he had associated with her once upon a time, Melissa thought fiercely. Even if he couldn't remember it.

Hoping that her fitted black dress and fake-pearl earrings fitted the bill, she felt almost dizzy as she approached him and even dizzier when he lifted his head and looked at her. He was wearing some kind of charcoal-grey suit, which fitted his muscular body to perfection, a soft ivory silk shirt and a tie in an understated shade of beaten-gold.

He didn't get up—just gave a businesslike nod of his dark head in greeting and then a narrow-eyed glance at the maître d' who instantly slipped away, as if that was what he had been briefed to do. You would never have thought that she and this golden-eyed man had been lovers, thought Melissa, with a sudden terrible wave of sadness.

'Sit down,' he said.

'Thanks.'

Indicating the drinks which were already cluttering up the table, Casimiro raised his dark eyebrows in question. 'I've taken the liberty of ordering the food and wine. We need to talk and I don't want to be disrupted by an endless series of sommeliers and waiters. I hope you don't have any objections to that?'

She wondered what he'd do if she said yes. That she wanted nothing more than to hear a five-minute spiel about the 'dish of the day' or spend minutes in a glory of indecision while she made the impossible choice of what wonderful food to eat. But you didn't object when a king chose your meal for you, did you? She doubted whether anyone had objected to anything in his whole privileged life. And her appetite had practically disappeared anyway.

'That's fine.'

'You'd like some wine?'

She thought of the dangers of wine and the way it softened your perception of the world. The slow creep of intoxication and then the even greater danger of staring across the table into the deep golden gleam of his eyes and remembering the way he'd made love to her on the sofa…

She felt her cheeks redden. *He didn't* make love to you—*he had quick and emotionless sex with you*, she reminded herself painfully. *He made you feel worthless—and wine is the last thing in the world you need*.

'Just water for me, thanks,' she said quietly, picking up the already poured glassful and swallowing some quickly—even though it seemed to have little effect on the parchment-like sensation in her throat.

Sipping some Petrus from his own glass, Casimiro studied her across the flickering candlelight. 'I've had the test result,' he said slowly.

'And?' Even as she said it Melissa wondered why she was bothering to ask when she knew exactly what the answer would be. Probably for the same reason that she had let that middle-aged doctor poke around in Ben's mouth with a swab yesterday morning. Because ever since she had told Casimiro about his son, she seemed to have lost control of her own life. Well, wasn't it time to start taking some of that control back?

'It's positive,' he said. 'Ninety-nine point nine per cent positive, in fact.'

'You should have listened to me and saved yourself the money.'

Casimiro's eyes narrowed. 'Is that supposed to be a joke?'

'It's not really a joking matter, is it?'

His frown deepened. He had expected—what? Some kind of *relief* that he had acknowledged the paternity claim. Maybe even some gratitude. When instead she was sitting there with what looked suspiciously like defiance flashing from her green eyes.

'We have to decide now what to do,' he said heavily.

Melissa opened her mouth to reply but at that moment a plate of grilled fish and salad was placed on the table in front of each of them—and a basket of warm bread offered. She shook her head and waited until the waiter had gone before staring at Casimiro.

'What do you mean, "do"?'

His eyes narrowed. 'What did you think would happen next? When it was proved that I was the child's father?'

'Ben,' she said hotly. 'His name is Ben.'

'What did you think would happen?' he repeated.

Melissa stared down at the feathery little bits of dill which were decorating her plate before looking up at him again, steeling herself against the accusation sparking from his golden eyes. 'I thought you'd want to see him from time to time.'

He gave a short and bitter laugh. 'What, just slot in and out of his life occasionally? And no doubt write you a big fat cheque so you could up your standard of living.'

'I told you in the beginning that I wasn't motivated by money and I meant every word of it. What is more, I don't have to stay and listen to your insults, Casimiro.'

'Oh, but I'm afraid that you do,' he demurred, in a low, silky voice. 'Try throwing a scene in here and you will regret it. The restaurant is owned by a friend of mine and the car in which you travelled is at my disposal. They won't take you anywhere without my instructions, and it's a long way to walk back to that...' he seemed to struggle with a word to describe it '...apartment you live in.'

The subtle dig about her home was the last straw—because didn't he realise how difficult it had been for her to manage on a salary like hers? No, he probably didn't realise and even if he did—he probably wouldn't care.

For a moment she felt like defying him. Like jumping up and running out and flagging down a car to take her home as fast as possible. But she couldn't do that. She was a mother and responsible, not only for her own safety—but for that of her child. And besides, you couldn't run away from things just because they made you feel uncomfortable. You had to stand your ground and face them—no matter how arrogant and unfeeling the person you were dealing with.

'Is that why you brought me here?' she demanded. 'So that I would be a captive audience?'

'Partly, yes.' But there had been other reasons. The risk of him being seen visiting her apartment twice in one week was too great. Someone wanting to earn themselves some extra money could easily tip off one of the tabloids. Yes, the car he had travelled in had been unmarked, but the presence of bodyguards always alerted the general public to someone of money and substance.

And hadn't he wanted to see her in a setting somewhere outside his home—or hers? Somewhere neutral. To view her objectively, as it were. To see how she might fit in if she was outside her comfort zone. His eyes skated over her consideringly, acknowledging that she didn't look too bad despite the fake jewellery and the unremarkable dress. But then she did have magnificently thick hair, he conceded—as well as a pair of remarkably green eyes.

'What do you suggest we do?' she questioned, wishing that he wouldn't look at her like that—in that cool and calculating way—and wishing even more that her body wouldn't prickle with response to his lazy assessment.

'We will have to marry,' he said flatly.

'*Marry?*'

The heavy silver fork with which she had just been about to attack the fish—more in a polite gesture to the chef than because she had really wanted it—fell to her plate with a loud clatter and as if by magic a waiter suddenly appeared, his face wreathed in concern. But Casimiro waved him away impatiently, his face darkening with fury because her reaction did not bode well. Hadn't he expected—wanted—some kind of fawning gratitude from her?

'Must you show your emotions so openly?' he snapped.

Melissa gave a bitter laugh. 'Maybe my acting skills aren't as accomplished as yours.'

'And what's that supposed to mean?'

She shook her head. 'It doesn't matter.'

'Oh, but it does,' he objected. 'Tell me. I insist.'

For a moment she felt like retorting that he might be King but he didn't have the power to get her to do something she didn't want to. Except that deep down she suspected her words might lack conviction. And maybe it would do him *good* to hear a few home truths for once.

'When I met you—you seemed like—well, like a…'

She chose her words carefully because the last thing she wanted him to hear was how completely he had captivated her heart in those few heady days of their romance. Because even if he had lost his memory, she wasn't stupid enough to think it had been mutual. For her, it had been a life-changing experience. And for him? Nothing more than an agreeable affair with no questions asked. 'You seemed like a nice guy,' she finished.

Casimiro recoiled as if he had been struck. '*A nice guy?*' he repeated incredulously. 'You are trying to damn me with faint praise?'

'Oh, what's the point in raking up all this?' she questioned tiredly. 'It doesn't matter what I say—all I know is that, whatever happens, we can't get married.'

His eyes narrowed. 'Why not?'

'Because we don't love each other—why, we don't even *like* each other!'

Her insolence and thanklessness almost took his breath away—but he would wait until he had his ring on her finger before he attempted to show her just what he would and would not tolerate.

'We have a child between us,' he reminded her. 'A child who is the rightful heir to my throne. A throne that I was about to renounce,' he added bitterly, the words out before he could stop them.

Across the candlelight, Melissa stared at him. '*Renounce* your kingdom? But why would you do that?'

'Because I felt trapped,' he snapped. 'Unable to live my life as I wished to live it. And my brother also has a son—which is why I was about to relinquish my kingdom to him.'

'B-but you've always been heir to the throne,' said Melissa shakily, trying to assemble all the facts which were jumbling together in her mind. 'You must have been used to the restrictions it put on you.'

Of course he had. But he had been able to temporarily forget about those restrictions when he had been living his life to the full. Galloping his beloved horse, or taking out his little sailing boat and skimming it around the island. Or scaling one of the mighty peaks of the Prassino range of mountains over on the eastern side of Zaffirinthos.

But after his fall, everything had changed and his 'dangerous' activities had been curtailed. The people had nearly lost their beloved King, they had argued passionately—and he must ensure that he did not place himself in such a vulnerable position again.

Casimiro had been able see their point—even if he had not necessarily agreed with it. So that when his brother's wife had given birth to baby Cosimo, it had occurred to him that he could give his people what they surely desired more than anything. A continuation of the royal bloodline. And his throne to a brother who had always secretly wanted it. And then along had come Miss Melissa Maguire and put paid to all his plans.

He stared into her green eyes, at the spiky shadows made by her long lashes. 'Because since my accident so much has been forbidden to me that I feel hemmed in,' he said grimly. 'Like the bird about to soar up into the sky suddenly being shut in a gilded cage. Trapped.'

Melissa swallowed, because—despite his hateful arrogance—she could hear an awful kind of emptiness in his voice. And something in her heart went out to him—made her want to offer him comfort even though he would probably just fling it back in her face. 'But won't you feel even more restricted if you have to get married just because you've got a baby?' she whispered.

His eyes became shuttered. 'I have no choice in the matter.'

'No choice?' she echoed, unsure of what he meant. 'Surely everyone has a choice—even kings?'

'Oh, how naïve you are, Melissa!' he mocked softly. 'Zaffirinthian law dictates that no abdication can be made while there is a living direct heir. So, you see, your revelation about...Ben...means that I am no longer free to renounce my throne.'

She realised instantly—as perhaps he had intended her to realise—that she had effectively trapped him as well. That the baby was yet another bar in the gilded cage he had spoken of. And as Ben's mother, so was she.

And trapping him was the last thing she had wanted, or wished for. Yes, he had been harsh and cruel in the wake of her revelation—but, in spite of the pain it had caused her, she could understand his reaction. Yes, he was arrogant and uncaring, but once she had adored him—and she had never set out to snare him. She felt the telltale prickle of tears to her eyes.

'I'm sorry, Casimiro,' she whispered. 'So very sorry.'

It was the bright glimmer of tears which did it. Tears which made her eyes look as bright and as brilliant as emeralds. And their brilliant gleam—combined with the faint lilac of her scent—took him back to a place he'd thought he'd left for ever. The memory which had stubbornly stayed in the depths of his mind now rose to the surface, like a bubble of air set free.

Emerald stars, he thought. He had once told her that her eyes were like *emerald stars*.

He stared into her face. 'I've remembered,' he said coldly.

CHAPTER SEVEN

THROUGH the flickering gleam of candlelight, Melissa
saw the dawning comprehension in Casimiro's eyes.

'Remembered what?' she questioned breathlessly.

He rubbed his fingertip against the scar at his temple
and for one brief moment he felt intense relief as his
memory came flooding back, as if someone had just
lifted a heavy weight from his shoulders. 'You. Us.' *She
had been telling the truth all along*, he realised. She was
not just some woman on the make. Not some kind of
'crazy' who was stalking him. She was a woman with
whom he had enjoyed a brief and heady affair—but one
which had never been meant to endure.

And now? Now their destinies were entwined whether
he liked it or not—but let them both be clear about the
reality, lest she spin fairy-tale fantasies as women were
so prone to do. 'Except that there wasn't really an "us",
was there, Melissa? We met at an after-show party and
it happened very quickly after that. What was it, three
days—or four? I hardly think our few hours of snatched
sex would qualify as a grand romance, do you?'

A few hours of snatched sex. It was as if her memory of that time had been a delicate and intricate glass
structure she'd carefully preserved—and Casimiro had

smashed it without thought or care. Melissa threw her napkin down over the fast-congealing fish and began to get up.

'Sit down!' he ordered.

'No, I won't sit down! I don't care if I have to walk all the way home—I will not sit here and be insulted by you!'

He could see that she meant it. He could also see the maître d' hovering anxiously over in the doorway, but a faint shake of Casimiro's head was enough to dispatch him. For a moment he was torn between fury at her outrageous insubordination—and a grudging respect for her spirit. 'Sit down, Melissa.' He met the unwavering resistance in her eyes. 'Please.'

Perhaps it was the unexpectedness of his appeal which made Melissa hesitate—or perhaps it was just the acknowledgement that this was not a word with which he was familiar. She doubted whether kings had to say 'please' very much in the normal run of events—and what kind of example was that to set to Ben, who she was determined was going to have the best manners in the world?

Melissa sank back down into the chair, secretly relieved to rest the suddenly shaky legs which she doubted would carry her outside, let alone all the way home. It was all so much of a shock. Everything. The test result and his reaction to it. Yes, of course she had known that there could only be one possible candidate for the role of father to her baby—but she hadn't been expecting this great swamp of emotion. She had bottled up her secret for so long that she felt quite shaky now that it was all out in the open.

'You've remembered *everything*?' she whispered.

He shrugged. 'For what it's worth.' Yet the missing piece of memory came as a huge relief—as if he had been made complete once more. And, reluctantly, he allowed himself to fill in some detail on their affair. He remembered the taste of freedom he'd felt with her. The heady sensation of feeling normal—and the subsequent feeling of emptiness when he had returned to the restrictions of his kingdom. He had felt like a condemned man being given his last meal and knowing he would never eat again.

'Do you...do you regret it?' she questioned.

The emotional gates which had briefly swung open now slammed shut. 'Regrets are a waste of time,' he said icily. 'We need to discuss what we're going to do—and the most pressing matter is our marriage, which must take place as soon as possible.'

Melissa stared at the cold hauteur of his features and for the first time she realised that the man she had adored no longer existed. Perhaps he never had. Perhaps it had just been a temporary role he had occupied while they'd been lovers. And could she really bear to be shackled to this cold-faced king for the rest of her life? She shook her head. 'I'm not going to marry you.'

'I'm afraid that's non-negotiable, Melissa.'

Melissa's breath seemed to catch in her throat. 'You can't *say* something like that,' she whispered.

'I can, because it happens to be true.'

'You can't actually *force* me to marry you—what, drag me screaming and kicking down the aisle?' She fixed him with a look she hoped concealed the fear which was fast growing inside her. That he could do with her exactly what he wanted. 'I don't imagine that would do your image much good.'

'No, I can't force you—but I can take your son from you.'

Melissa froze as the world seemed to grow dark. It was the single most effective and terrifying threat he could have made—and the fact that he had uttered it made her want to lash out at him. 'You can't do that, either.'

'You really think so? I wonder if you're prepared to test the full might of the King against a single mother of your standing.'

'There's nothing *wrong* with my standing!'

'Do you consider it appropriate that the heir to the throne should be brought up in this way?'

'He's clean and well fed and stimulated and—*happy*!' she defended.

'And his home? You think that is a good place in which to bring up a royal Prince?'

It was the first time she'd actually thought of Ben as a Prince and, although the mother in her thrilled with pride, the title terrified her as well. Because didn't it seem an awfully *distancing* thing—to be a royal Prince? Especially since *she* was just a commoner...

'We don't have to stay living there if you think it's so awful!' she declared wildly, because the expression which was darkening his arrogant features was really beginning to unsettle her.

'You mean you'd let me buy you somewhere bigger?' he suggested softly.

She walked straight into it. 'If that's what you want.'

'Ah! So you don't mind accepting my money, after

all, Melissa? A remarkable change of heart. How come I'm not surprised?'

Now he was making her sound like some kind of cheap gold-digger. Twisting everything she uttered so that she felt as if she were in some sort of verbal maze—with everything she said leading nowhere. 'I thought that's what you wanted,' she said, in confusion.

'No, it is *not* what I want!' he snapped. 'I can just imagine what outcome buying you a big place and settling you with a suitable income would produce. Why, you'd have every male in the vicinity sniffing around you as if all their Christmases had come at once!'

'You're disgusting!'

'No, Melissa—I am being practical. Make a woman rich and she becomes a target.'

'And make her poor and she becomes a puppet?' she retorted.

At this he gave a glimmer of a smile and leaned back in his chair—and maybe he had given some kind of sign to the staff because their untouched plates of fish were whisked away and Melissa's glass of water refreshed.

It was time to call her bluff, he thought.

'Okay. Have it your way.' He laced his long fingers together and Melissa saw the shiny gold signet ring glinting on his little finger. 'No marriage—if that's what you want.'

Now she felt as if she were in a hall of mirrors—where reality was distorted differently every time she tried to examine it. Melissa frowned. 'But...but...you just said it was non-negotiable.'

'And you charmingly responded by implying that I would have to drag you down the aisle.' His eyes tossed her a silent, mocking challenge. 'I agree, not exactly the best public relations exercise for Zaffirinthos. So we won't get married and obviously I *will* have to make some kind of financial provision for Ben. You'll need to live somewhere secure—because once it comes out that he's a royal baby you will be subjected to all kinds of inducements and attempts to exploit that.'

'From *crazies*?' she echoed sarcastically.

Oh, but her defiance and her sharp tongue inflamed him! Would make his inevitable victory all the sweeter. 'That's right.' Leaning back in his chair, he studied her. 'And, naturally, we'll have to draw up some kind of legal settlement.'

'Settlement?' A sense of wariness began to creep over her.

'Of course.' He sent her a look of cool challenge. 'While Ben can never be acknowledged as my *legal* heir because he is illegitimate—nonetheless I still wish to have an equal say in his upbringing.'

It was the word *illegitimate* which leapt out at her like a dark spectre. An old-fashioned word which wasn't used much any more because having a baby out of wedlock was no longer considered shameful in the way it had been in the bad old days. But Casimiro was making it *sound* shameful. Was that deliberate? she wondered.

'Equal say?' she repeated, swallowing down the terrible nameless fear which was beginning to well up inside her.

'Well, that *is* only fair, Melissa—and supremely modern. And presumably what you want.'

She was tempted to tell him not to presume anything about her but backbiting was a luxury she could ill afford—not when she was desperately trying to keep her wits about her. Because it felt as if he was playing some kind of cruel and sophisticated game with her only he hadn't bothered to tell her the rules. Had he really said that he wanted to be fair and modern? Why, he was the least fair and modern man she'd ever met!

'Ben will need to spend time with me,' he continued. 'And of course, much of his schooling will need to be done on the island.'

'His *schooling*?'

'Where else will he learn to become fluent in Greek and Italian?' questioned Casimiro sardonically. 'In Walton-on-Thames? He will also need to understand the island's culture since it is his heritage. Because when I *do* marry, any legitimate son I may have will inherit the crown—but Ben will always be able to play a significant role within the kingdom. If he wants to.'

Everything he had said to her was like being slapped in the face with a cold fish, but one phrase hit her with greater force than any other. So hard, it made her feel as if she were reeling from the impact. 'M-marry?'

Casimiro understood perfectly the stuttered and horrified word for he knew that a woman's jealousy should never be underestimated. 'If I'm staying on Zaffirinthos—which now I must—then I will need a wife.' He smiled. 'And in a way, your refusal to marry me has liberated me. This way, I'll be able to find myself someone who's much more suitable. Someone who will care for and love Ben when he is staying with us.'

That did it. There were many disadvantages to bringing up a child on your own, but one of the benefits was that you didn't have to share them—or not be able to see them 24/7. Melissa thought of another woman with Ben—being a pretend mother to him when she wasn't around. Tucking him up at bedtimes and holding onto his chubby little hand. Perhaps even witnessing his first faltering steps or hearing him stumble out new words. Her son enjoying a parallel life which didn't include *her*. Nausea rose in her throat and threatened to choke her. *Anything* would be better than that. Even marriage to Casimiro.

She looked at him across the table, some inner voice urging her to stay calm—because what if he turned round and told her that it was too late and he'd changed his mind?

'Actually, Casimiro—when I come to think of it—perhaps I was a little…well, *hasty*.' Her fingers fluttered to the base of her throat where she could feel the mad racing of a pulse. 'And perhaps, well, what I'm trying to say is that I *would* like to marry you, after all.'

He waited for a moment, just long enough to see anxiety cloud those bright green eyes—and then Casimiro lifted the linen napkin to his lips to hide his smile of triumph.

CHAPTER EIGHT

MELISSA'S whole life changed from the moment she agreed to marry Casimiro. One minute she was struggling to pay the bills and the next she was deciding whether a white wedding would be hypocritical. She tried telling herself that it was the same for every newly engaged woman—but deep down she knew that her experience was entirely different.

Most women weren't tearing out their roots and moving to an unknown land—a Mediterranean island where she was to be crowned Queen. And most women wouldn't need to undergo a dramatic change of image before they walked down the aisle. To 'look the part'—as Casimiro unemotionally informed her during that tense ride back to her apartment, after the fraught dinner when she'd agreed to be his wife.

'I won't make any kind of announcement until you're ready, Melissa. Otherwise you won't know a moment's peace. The circus will start soon enough.'

One word had jarred—along with the fact that he had been sitting on the far side of the car seat as if to emphasise the great gulf between them. *'Ready?'*

He had turned to her, his face a series of shifting shadows combined with the occasional illumination of a street light as the powerful car travelled towards her home.

'But of course. You need to be prepared—and for that you will need an entirely new wardrobe. New everything, in fact—everything that will befit a queen. As will…' He had scowled. 'Why on earth did you call him Ben?'

This had made Melissa bristle with indignation and hurt. 'What's wrong with it? My maternal grandfather was called Benjamin—it's a lovely name!'

'It is not the name of a king!'

'Funny as it may seem, I wasn't actually thinking about his enthronement when I was giving birth to him!' She had been too scared at the enormity of what was happening and what lay ahead. Even when she had clutched the wet and shiny newborn to her breast she had wondered if she would ever be able to support him properly. Party planning wasn't the most secure career option in the book—everyone knew that.

Well, at least she now knew that Ben would never go short of anything—but at what price?

'My brother's wife, Catherine—she will accompany you on a shopping trip,' Casimiro had continued. 'As a royal princess herself, she will know exactly what it is you require.'

'So you've…you've told her that we're engaged?'

'We are not yet formally engaged, Melissa—not until I put the ring on your finger. Xaviero and Catherine have been informed that we are to marry, yes—but that was mainly out of courtesy. Nobody else knows. Not yet.'

Melissa had nodded and blurted out a still shell-shocked goodnight as the chauffeur opened the door of the limousine. And the next day she was as nervous as a kitten as she waited for Princess Catherine by the perfume section in one of London's glitziest department stores, as arranged.

She didn't know what she had been expecting—maybe a rash of security guards crawling all over the place, a bit like the grand ball in Zaffirinthos. As it was, a petite and beautiful whirlwind of a woman appeared without any fuss or fanfare and embraced her as if they were old friends. Dressed in a simple cotton dress, her blonde hair scraped back in a ponytail, she didn't look at all like a princess. Only the clutch of diamond bands which sparkled on her wedding finger gave any indication of her wealth or position.

'Oh, it's always easy to go around London incognito,' she confided to Melissa as they headed straight for the designer floor of the store. 'Though not so easy on Zaffirinthos, of course—which is one of the reasons we like living here in England. Although I have to admit that Xaviero got awfully homesick when we were there for the ball. Here.' She scooped an armful of evening dresses off one of the rails. 'You'll need loads of these.'

It seemed to Melissa that she needed loads of everything—skirts, blouses, day-dresses, cocktail dresses, shoes, boots and handbags—and every single garment was made in the most costly fabric and to the highest possible standard. She didn't think she'd ever worn real silk before and now it seemed it was going to be the exclusive fabric for the underwear and nightwear which she tried on with the guidance of an assistant while Catherine had a bubbling telephone conversation with her husband. Blushing, she remembered Casimiro's cruel jibes when he'd seen her in her baggy T-shirt and wondered if he might approve of these.

They didn't even have to carry any of the numerous bags home—because Catherine ordered for them to be dispatched directly to Melissa's apartment.

'You can sort them out from there,' she said breezily as they travelled by limousine to the fancy Granchester Hotel, where they were shown a window table overlooking the park and where afternoon tea was laid out. 'And get rid of all your old stuff while you're at it.'

As she was offered a choice between Lapsong or Earl Grey tea Melissa suddenly felt like a fraud. This woman was going to be her sister-in-law—was she going to have to pretend to be something she wasn't? And would Catherine be quite so friendly if she knew the truth about her?

'I don't...I don't have very much room at home,' she admitted. 'It's just...just a tiny place.'

Catherine looked at her. 'I know it is,' she said softly. 'And I also know about your doubts and your fears because I've had them, too. You see, I was a chambermaid when I met and fell in love with my husband.'

Melissa dropped her gaze to the dainty little sandwich which lay on her plate—terrified that Catherine would see the truth in her eyes. Because there hadn't been any falling in love with her and Casimiro. Nor anything like it. In fact, how had he so charmingly described it? Oh, yes—as 'a few hours of snatched sex'. What kind of a basis was that for a marriage—any marriage—let alone one where they would be the focus of so many eyes?

Catherine leaned across the table and squeezed her

hand. 'You'll be *fine*. It's just wonderful to think I'm going to have a sister-in-law who's English, too—and that you will make Casimiro as happy as Xav and I have been.' She lowered her voice. 'To be honest, we were really worried—for a while back there it looked like Casimiro wouldn't find the right woman at all, and Xaviero got this funny feeling that he might be about to renounce the throne.'

'Really?' questioned Melissa tentatively. 'Did they talk about it?'

'Oh, no. As brothers they've never really communicated that much.' Catherine looked at her with hopeful aquamarine eyes. 'But maybe that will all change now. There's nothing like marriage to soften the heart of a hard man.'

Melissa didn't like to disillusion Catherine by telling her that there was unlikely to be any softening effect from her own cold-blooded union with the King. And could he really have been planning to abdicate in favour of his brother without even bothering to *tell* him? Surely even he couldn't be that arrogant? But then she thought about the clever and cold-blooded way he had manipulated her into marrying him and she thought that maybe he could.

The following day she took Ben to the same shop and kitted him out with a wardrobe fit for a prince. She enjoyed this expedition much more—because this was every mother's dream and her curly-headed son soon had all the shop assistants eating out of his hand.

The hardest part of leaving was saying goodbye to her aunt Mary, who received the news that her niece was about to become a queen with remarkable composure, congratulating Melissa and telling her that she'd lived too long to be surprised by anything. But she was going to miss Ben, of course.

'I do wish you'd come out to Zaffirinthos,' Melissa said with soft yearning in her voice, knowing she could never tell her beloved aunt the truth behind Casimiro's cruel marital ultimatum. 'Come out and look after Ben and let me look after you.'

'And sure aren't I coming out to help when you marry that handsome King of yours?'

'I meant after that. Permanently. You could have a wonderful life there, Auntie—I know you could.'

But Aunt Mary had been adamant. She had seen too many marriages get off to a bad start because of the interference from older relatives, she said. And besides—what would she do all day in a great big palace?

People are intimidated by the life I am entering, Melissa realised as she waited in her little apartment for Casimiro to collect her. He was taking her from her old life to the new and unknown one which awaited her on Zaffirinthos. And where the King was that night recording a television broadcast to his nation. For he had decided that the only way to present their wedding to the world was openly and honestly. To tell his people that he took his responsibilities seriously—and to introduce them to his son and bride-to-be.

There was a tap at the door and she pulled it open to find Casimiro standing there. He was wearing a dark suit which looked terribly formal and had instructed her to dress in something 'suitable for a royal engagement'. She had taken Catherine's advice on what this should be, but now she wasn't too sure.

The cut of the green brocade dress and matching jacket was more severe than her usual style and the accompanying jade shoes a little high. So high, in fact, that they made her tower. She was a tall woman anyway, and most men would have been dwarfed by the additional height—though not Casimiro. But these put her almost at eye-level to him. Tall enough to look into the cool golden gleam of his eyes—and to realise just how emotionless those eyes were.

She saw him look down at Ben, who was sitting on a blanket bashing a wooden spoon against an old saucepan in an apartment he would never see again. All bound for his new life in smart little navy shorts and an embroidered poplin shirt—his curls looking like a shiny black mop.

'Doesn't he look gorgeous?' she said, her voice choked with quiet pride and the sudden savage wrench she felt at having to say goodbye to England.

Casimiro glanced down at the infant, who was oblivious to the machinations of the adults around him. Whose life would never be the same again. He was making some primitive-sounding singing noises as he banged the spoon against the metal. His perfect skin had a faint olive tinge to it and you could see the chubby symmetry of each tiny limb. How was it possible that this child had sprung from his loins? Casimiro wondered disbelievingly as he felt a strange clenching sensation around his heart.

Melissa watched them. For a moment, Casimiro seemed about to step forward—something in his body language suggesting that he might be about to pick Ben up—and Melissa willed him to make contact. *Touch your son*, she urged him silently—*touch your son and begin to love him.* But the moment passed and he seemed to change his mind, lifting his gaze to her instead. A gaze which seemed to her to contain nothing other than slightly cool censure.

'He'll need to get his hair cut before the wedding,' he said.

Hot tears threatened to spring to her eyes, but she blinked them away before they'd had a chance to form. Of all the things to say at the beginning of this new life with his son! It had sounded like a criticism of both Ben *and* her. *He will not cut his curls*, thought Melissa fiercely—but even she could see that having a row just before she stepped into the public spotlight was a bad idea.

Instead she conjured up a faltering smile from somewhere and drew a deep breath. 'So…this is it?'

'This is it.' He looked down into her pale, heart-shaped face—against which her eyes looked intensely green. Her lips were parted and gleaming, as if they wanted to be kissed, and suddenly he thought about all the many pleasurable opportunities that this marriage would bring with it. He would be able to make love to her over and over again, he realised—as many times as he wanted. As many times as she wanted…

Leaning forward, he grazed his mouth almost negligently over hers, feeling her own tremble against the brush of his flesh. For a moment he kissed her deeply until he heard her make a broken little sigh, and when he pulled away from her it was to see the unmistakable disappointment which had clouded her eyes.

'Oh,' she whispered, unable to keep the note of frustration from her voice.

As a demonstration of his power over her, it was perfect. Casimiro smiled—even though he was aching to possess her once more. 'Didn't you scold me the other day for trying to make love to you while our son slept next door?' he chided softly.

Instead, he withdrew a leather box from his pocket and flipped open the lid to reveal a diamond solitaire ring of such startling clarity and brilliance that for a moment Melissa couldn't quite believe her eyes.

'Is it real?' She forced the joke out like trying to squeeze the last little bit of toothpaste from the tube, but there was no answering smile on his face.

'Oh, it's the real thing,' he answered unevenly—because even he couldn't deny its emotional significance. 'It was my mother's engagement ring.'

'Your mother's?' A moment of memory took her right back to a time when he'd caught her crying over her own mother, when he'd offered her a lift to stop the rain getting in her cheap shoes. What wouldn't she give for a moment like that now—in exchange for all the glittering jewels in the world?

'A rare Calistan diamond,' he continued, concentrating on the gem rather than on her question as he prised it from its velvet claws. 'De-flawless and perfect. You will never wear fake jewellery again, Melissa.'

But a chill passed over her heart as he slid the ring onto her trembling finger. She was about to get married to a man who saw her simply as a commodity—and it occurred to Melissa that she'd never felt so fake in her whole life.

CHAPTER NINE

'You look beautiful,' he murmured. 'As beautiful as any bride on her wedding morning.'

Melissa turned round from the mirror to see Casimiro standing in the doorway of her sumptuous suite of palace rooms—a formidable and commanding presence in his Zaffirinthian naval uniform.

Medals gleamed at his chest and the dark livery drew attention to his imposing frame and powerful presence. Her eyes blinked rapidly—as if she still couldn't quite believe that she was marrying this man and that within a couple of hours they would be man and wife. Or, rather, King and Queen. She kept thinking that in a minute she would wake up and she and Ben would find themselves back in Walton in their tiny apartment with the spluttering shower and the barking dogs outside.

'You're...you're not supposed to be here!' she stumbled.

He raised his dark brows. 'Why not?'

'Because it isn't traditional for the groom to see his bride on the morning of the wedding!'

'I hardly think we're a shining example of traditionalism, do you, Melissa?' he questioned wryly.

Anxiously, she glanced around. Where were the maids

who'd been helping her—scurrying around making un-necessary adjustments to the restrained silk of her wed-ding suit? 'Where's everyone gone?'

'I sent them away.'

She lifted her eyes to his, aware that the unaccus-tomed weight of several layers of mascara was making them feel very heavy. 'Why?'

'Because I wanted to see you. Before the marriage. Alone.'

Melissa's heart began beating very fast. She had tried to tell herself that this marriage was wrong on all kinds of levels. When doubts had come to her—mainly in the middle of the night—she had convinced herself that she would be insane not to go through with it. That mainly she was doing it for Ben—so that he wouldn't be wrenched away from her. So that he wouldn't grow up as a part-time royal who might one day push her away completely.

But although Ben was a valid enough reason for this marriage—she was doing it for someone else too. For herself. For the stupid craving and yearning part of her which had never stopped loving this man and wanting to know him better. Hoping that once he had slipped the wedding band on her finger he might allow her to see beneath the formidable exterior he presented to the world. Would it be possible to chip away at the ice and maybe rediscover the warmth of the man she had once known? Would he give her that chance? Or had that man disappeared altogether—leaving nothing but this beautiful yet icy shell which stood before her now in his uniform?

'Why alone?' she breathed. 'Are you having…second thoughts?'

'Are you?'

'No.' She searched his face for a glimmer of affection—some kind of regard—but all she could see was a telltale darkening at the depths of the amber eyes. 'I…I am prepared to go through with it. I want to be a good wife.'

'How dutiful you sound, Melissa.'

'Well, isn't this all about duty?' she questioned quietly. 'Yours to your country and mine to my son?'

Her logic took his breath away, for it was a quality he looked for in his advisors but had not expected from her. Hadn't he expected—and wanted—some kind of soft and melting acquiescence? A very feminine capitulation to the allure of wealth and high office he was offering her and which might have made her show a little more *gratitude*?

But no. There was nothing soft or melting about Melissa Maguire today. She looked, he thought—like some sort of ice-Queen.

Advised by his aides that a white wedding would be highly inappropriate in the circumstances, instead she wore a muted suit of beaten silver—the colour of some untouched glacier. Mahogany hair had been piled into an intricate confection on top of her head and left unadorned—for she would be crowned during the wedding ceremony itself.

Yet it was her face which startled him. The green eyes were edged in black and her lips gleamed a faint rose-pink colour. A professional make-up artist had been presented with the raw material of this unrefined woman from a small town in England—and a sleek, almost un-recognisable beauty had emerged.

He thought how well she had dealt with the press—doing nothing other than smiling in just about every shot he had seen of her. That and holding their son tightly—who had also looked particularly angelic, even if Melissa had stubbornly refused to have his hair trimmed before the press call.

The photographers had demanded that the couple kiss and then that Casimiro lift up his son—but he had refused both requests. How the hell could he act like a father for the cameras when he didn't feel remotely like a father inside? Or, indeed, a loving bridegroom.

What he *did* feel like was a frustrated lover and now he ran his eyes over the slim lines of her silver-clothed body.

'Very beautiful,' he repeated silkily.

'Thank you.'

'A dutiful response, too,' he mocked.

'To a dutiful comment,' she retorted, because if she was to be his Queen then she would learn her lessons well. And what was the accusation he had hurled at her in the restaurant? The one that had stuck? Oh, yes. *Must you show your emotions so openly?* Well, that was a mistake she would not be making again in a hurry. She would be his cool and collected consort. She would make him proud that she was his Queen.

'But I meant it,' he said softly. 'Though I think you would be more beautiful still if you were stripped naked and lying in my bed right now.'

Melissa felt the quickening of her heart. Perhaps if tender words of affection had preceded it, then she might

have just taken this as an erotic declaration from her very
virile groom. But there had been no tenderness—and so
his comment came out sounding like a boast of arrogant
possession. Like a man who'd just bought a new sports
car and was longing to try it out.

'We'll have our honeymoon for all that,' she said,
and then bit her lip. 'I do hope Ben will be okay while
we're gone.'

'Of course he will. He'll be with your aunt. And it's
only for one night, Melissa—surely that doesn't fall into
the category of child neglect.'

'Yes, I know. I know. But all this…' She waved a
satin-clad arm to encompass all the jewelled splendour
of her dressing room and then shrugged her shoulders
in what felt like a gesture of defeat. 'Well, it isn't really
what he's used to.'

He was tempted to say that it was a big improvement
on what Ben was used to, but even he could see that
wasn't the most diplomatic observation to make moments before they made their wedding vows. 'You've
left him before, haven't you?' His eyes sparked out a
challenge. 'You had no qualms about leaving him behind
when you came to help with the catering at the ball.'

Reluctantly, Melissa nodded. 'Yes, I know.'

'And you look scared,' he observed softly. 'What's
the matter, Melissa—scared to be alone with me?'

She tried to blank the mockery in his golden eyes but
she could do nothing about the scudding of her heart.
'No. Of course not.'

But that wasn't strictly true. She *was* scared—of her
own feelings and wondering how she would be able to
keep them under control, especially when they were

having sex. And what about when they *weren't* being intimate? What did you do on your honeymoon with a man who was little more than a stranger?

The wedding passed in a blur. It felt a bit like one of those dreams where you found yourself in a place you shouldn't be. According to tradition, Casimiro did not have a best man but two 'supporters' who were Xaviero, naturally—and Orso, his aide who had been with him since both men had been teenagers.

Melissa herself had no bridesmaid nor matron of honour—even though several of her school friends would have leapt at the chance. But her solo walk down the aisle somehow reinforced the rather low-key aspect of the ceremony. And as Catherine confided— 'They seem to make a habit of having low-key weddings on Zaffirinthos!'

The golden-haired Princess sat next to Aunt Mary during the service, with both women trying to contain the squirming of Ben and Cosimo, who were both grabbing at each other's hair.

It was slightly scary when the jewel-encrusted crown was placed on Melissa's head and although she had practised using a weighted headpiece before the ceremony, she was still taken aback by the heaviness of the historic coronet. It was so weighty that she had to keep her head at a certain angle for fear that her head would tip to one side, as if she were drunk.

But despite all the uncertainties which danced like ghosts on the periphery of her mind, Melissa couldn't help but feel a great swell of pride as Casimiro slid the ring on her finger.

I'm doing this for Ben, she told herself fiercely. He and

Casimiro will learn to love each other—for how could they not? Who could fail to love the mop-headed and beautiful boy they'd formed between them? And maybe afterwards…wasn't there a chance that *something* might grow between her and Casimiro, too? If not love, then surely some kind of workable relationship.

To the celebratory peal of bells which rang out from the huge cathedral at Ghalazamba. Melissa could see the blur of faces of all the people packed into the square— and the realisation that they were calling out *her* name was a daunting one. But also an exhilarating one.

After picking at the lavish wedding breakfast, Melissa went to change from her wedding clothes. They were spending their honeymoon on the eastern side of the islands, at one of the vast estates owned by the royal family.

'Pine-clad mountains and clear turquoise seas,' murmured Casimiro as he twisted the ignition on the Range Rover he was driving himself. He shot her a glance as she clicked in her seat belt, noticing the set expression on her pale face and the seductive curve of her breasts outlined against her dress. His voice dipped with unmistakable longing. 'And our first opportunity for intimacy after that erotic incident on the sofa.'

'I'm…I'm…' Whatever she had been about to say temporarily disappeared from her mind because he had placed his hand over her bare knee. 'Casimiro!'

'What?' Leaning across, he brushed his mouth against hers and could feel the responding shiver in her body as he briefly slid his fingers over the silken skin of her inner thigh. 'Don't you like it? Mmm? Ah! *Grazie al cielo!* I can see that you *do* like it.'

Melissa closed her eyes as the most delicious feeling began to flood through her veins. She swallowed. 'I...I thought that your security people were following us.'

'They're *your* security as well from now on, *mia bella*. But there are blacked-out windows in this vehicle for a reason and that is to prevent prying eyes from peering in.'

'But even so—'

'Don't worry—I wasn't intending to make love to you on the seat of the car—no matter how much the prospect might appeal to me.' He laughed as he removed his hand and drove the car through the palace gates. 'Relax, Melissa,' he urged softly. 'Just relax.'

She did her best, watching as the beautiful scenery flashed by, with its great green mountains and sapphire sweeps of sea, until they reached the dramatic eastern shores of the island.

The villa was beyond her wildest expectations—a vast mansion of a place sitting in twelve acres of luscious land with a giant pool and scented gardens, leading down to a private stretch of beach. There was an enormous bedroom which had been made ready for Ben, his own playroom—and even a sandpit and a scaled-down swimming pool which stood close to the larger one.

The estate was remote and access was virtually impossible—reached by one anonymous and dusty road, policed by burly-looking guards and surrounded by dense pine forests. Casimiro's personal bodyguards were to be housed in their own small complex at some way from the main house, where the housekeeper and cook lived. Other staff were to travel in daily from the nearby village, as and when required.

'They have been instructed that we want as little inter-
vention as possible. That we want to be on our own,' said
Casimiro as he showed her around.

But Melissa found herself looking at him with sudden
perception—aware of the fundamental flaw in his statement.

He had talked about wanting to spend some time
on their own—but of course they would never *really*
be on their own. Not now. Not ever. Constant surveil-
lance came with the territory. Had that been why he had
embraced his relative anonymity with such enthusiasm
when she'd known him in England—the playing at being
'ordinary' perhaps adding an extra layer of excitement to
their brief affair? Yet she could see now that it had been
nothing but fantasy. A period of pretending which was
a million miles away from the life he usually lived.

Dinner had been laid out for them on one of the ter-
races which overlooked the pool and the floodlit gardens.
Beyond that was the sea—indigo-deep and occasionally
moving with a little lick of white wave—and the only
sound was the amplified buzz of a million cicadas.

On the balcony of their bedroom, dominated by a
bed the size of a football pitch, they stood in silence for
a moment before Casimiro pulled her into his arms as
she had been waiting for him to do since the moment
they'd arrived. And now that the moment was here, she
wasn't sure whether the sudden escalation of her heart
was due to anticipation or dread—or a bit of both.

Casimiro stared down at a face which looked paper-
pale in the moonlight. Her eyes were like a startled
fawn's and he was suddenly aware of the magnitude of
what they'd done and the tension on her face.

'Tired?' he questioned.

Actually, she was near worn out. Exhausted by the emotional and physical strain of the past few days and the thought of what lay ahead. But Melissa knew that this wasn't the answer Casimiro wanted to hear—and certainly not on a night like this. It might be setting a bad precedent to such a marriage as theirs if she started it with what was euphemistically known as a 'headache'.

Injecting her voice with enthusiasm, she smiled. 'No, not at all.'

'Liar,' he retorted softly. 'There are shadows as dark as the night-time sea beneath your eyes.'

'Are there?' She touched her fingertips to the delicate skin beneath her eyes. 'To be honest, they're probably just labouring under the weight of all this mascara they put on me.'

The absurdly inconsequential little feminine response—the detail of which would never normally have entered his radar—now made his lips curve into a smile. 'I'd noticed,' he said drily.

'You don't like it?'

'No man likes a woman to wear too much make-up. We prefer to drift along under the illusion that beauty is effortless.'

Beauty. He had called her beautiful earlier and it was not a word that Melissa was used to hearing—well, not when it was associated with her. Was it something that he felt obliged to say now that they were married—that if he repeated it often enough he might end up believing it? She wanted to tell him that he didn't have to. She knew that it was nothing other than a marriage of convenience and she was striving for some kind of workable union, not reaching for the stars. That she'd rather have truth than diplomatic compliments he didn't mean. But she might run the risk of sounding ungrateful if she did that, so she simply smiled.

'Thank you,' she said quietly.

He found something in her voice oddly soothing—like sinking into a soft feather bed after long, uncomfortable days on horseback. His gaze drifted down to the terrace below—where the table was decked with roses and tall candles stood waiting to be lit. The staff would be discreet, he knew that. He could even imagine what they had been told. *The King is on his honeymoon—so do not disturb him unnecessarily.*

But suddenly Casimiro didn't want to sit on a moon-washed terrace and be served course after course of food by shadowy figures. Was a little shared solitude too much to ask on his wedding night? 'Hungry?' he questioned.

'Not…not particularly.'

'Yet you hardly ate a thing during the wedding breakfast.'

She was both touched and surprised that he'd noticed—particularly as he'd been deep in conversation with the Italian Prime Minister for much of the meal. 'We can eat if you're hungry,' she said.

He stared at her—at the floaty dress she'd changed into, in a shade of dark purple like one of those indigo shadows which sometimes drifted across the moon. At the elaborate twists of her hair—like gleaming dark snakes coiled high on her head. And some deep yearning took hold of him—a desire for the lure of the uncomplicated past he had shared with her. When for a few brief and heady days he had been able to cast off the burden of responsibility.

'I'm not in the least bit hungry,' he said unsteadily. 'At least, not for food.' He saw her eyes widen, saw her obvious uncertainty—which was slightly bizarre under the circumstances and yet somehow completely understandable. 'We can have champagne up here, if that's what you'd like?'

Melissa would have welcomed the cold, fizzing taste of dry champagne and the corresponding warmth which would bubble through her veins and maybe make her relax a little. But champagne had all kinds of connotations and the main one was of celebration—and wouldn't that seem a bit contrived after a marriage of convenience?

She didn't want Casimiro to think she needed some kind of mild intoxication before she could bear to go to bed with him. Even though inside she felt a trembling which was like a kaleidoscope of butterflies fluttering around at the base of her stomach.

Lifting her hands to his shoulders, she moved her face close to his. 'No,' she whispered. 'I don't want a drink.'

'What do you want?'

'I'm…I'm not sure.'

'This?' He leaned forward and brushed his lips over hers and they tasted cool and sweet.

Mutely, she nodded, her grip on him growing tighter as she was swept away by the sheer beauty of that kiss. They stood like that for an age, their mouths exploring like first-time lovers and the poignancy of *that* did not escape her.

Feeling her shiver, he moved away, looking down at
her closed eyes, which fluttered open to look at him. He
began to take the clips from her hair. Five clips in all
he removed, until every strand of it had tumbled free—
mahogany and shining. Next, he slid down the long zip
of her dress, slipped it down over her pale shoulders until
it pooled to the ground in a silken whisper. And then he
stepped back to look at her, narrowing his eyes like a
connoisseur.

'Ah, that is better!' he breathed appreciatively. 'A vast
improvement, *mia bella*.'

She knew what he meant. He was comparing her to
the woman she had been before and acknowledging that
this silk-satin underwear came nowhere close to a baggy
old grey T-shirt. And yet, back then, she had surely felt
more true to herself than the pampered creature who
stood before him now.

Her breasts were encased in apricot silk-satin, edged
in finest lace—the kind of bra which you sometimes
saw sleek Hollywood blondes wearing in those ultra-
glossy magazines which sat on the top shelf of news-
agents. High-cut panties matched the bra and made
her already long legs seem endless. Yet the feel of
such butter-soft silk against her skin made her feel
decadent—and she guessed that was no bad way for a
woman to feel on her honeymoon. She glanced at him
from between slitted and heavy lashes—and the darkening of his eyes told her loud and clear just how much
he wanted her.

'Casimiro,' she whispered.

Reading the blatant hunger in that slanted glance she
sent him made him wonder briefly what it might be like

to take her there, on the balcony. For their mingling skin to be washed by the warmth of the moonlit night as they came together. But he thought of her soft cries echoing in the silent night and the flash of her diamond ring which might attract the attention of a long-range camera, or guard...

'Come here,' he said throatily, pulling her into his arms, and he picked her up and carried her into their bedroom. She seemed all coltish arms and legs as he laid her down on the bed and she reached up for him, her dark hair spilling back against the pillow.

'Kiss me,' she whispered. 'Kiss me again.'

It was a curiously intimate little command and as Casimiro lowered his head to hers once more he felt himself poised on the brink of some brand-new discovery. The sensation that a kiss could somehow take on a million different guises and that he had just discovered a brand-new variation.

But something in its subtle magic made him instinctively wary and, freeing himself from its disconcerting spell, he got up and moved away from the bed—gesturing to his shirt and trousers with a rueful expression. 'There is little point, *mia bella*, in you wearing very little and me wearing all *this*...now, is there?'

'No,' she said dully, watching him as he removed his clothes. Watching—as she knew she was supposed to watch and savour—this highly privileged striptease. The sight of his powerful body gradually becoming naked was more than a little intimidating. As was the formidable power of his arousal as it sprang free. And studying him amid the opulence of this magnificent suite, she couldn't help thinking back to when they'd first been lovers. Of Casimiro in her teeny little bedsit—with the row of terraced houses opposite and the cramped bed in which they'd lain, all tangled and sleepy.

Yet as he stepped out of silken boxer shorts and her eyes were drawn to the definition of his powerful thighs, she thought that, beneath all the splendour, surely he was essentially the same man? Even if he had hidden that oh-so-human side to him this time around. Was that because he was still angry that she had trapped him into a life he had already chosen to reject? And would he ever be able to let that go—to let her close to him as once he had?

Well, she would not help matters by imagining the worst or by clamming up. He had told her in no uncertain terms that it was inappropriate to show her emotions—but surely that didn't apply when they were in bed together?

'Come here,' she said softly, and opened her arms to him.

Her sweetness affected him more than he had bargained for. Casimiro didn't know what he had expected on their wedding night. Coyness or shyness perhaps. Maybe triumph—or even anger.

Instead, he got passion. Pure and unequivocal. Unrestrained gasps of pleasure as he thrust deep into her. The tight slick as he moved inside her with gathering pace and felt her orgasm swelling up until it could no longer be contained.

'Casimiro,' she breathed, clutching onto his shoulders and clinging to him as if he were her only rock in a wild and thrashing sea. 'Oh. Oh. *Oh!*'

He felt her buck beneath him and then he too was lost

in the mindless bliss of sexual fulfilment—taken by the tide, like a surfer riding the biggest wave of all. For a while afterwards he just lay there, his mind blissfully free of thought or timetable, idly stroking back damp strands of hair from her sweat-sheened brow.

'So how was it?' he questioned eventually as he felt the ecstatic trembling of her body quieten at last.

It took a moment before she had the composure to answer him.

'It?'

'The day. The wedding. The crowds and the cameras. You seemed...' his voice grew thoughtful as he considered her reaction to what must have been a bizarre experience '...remarkably composed.'

Melissa thought about it. 'It wasn't as bad as I thought it was going to be,' she admitted. 'To be honest, I was so busy worrying that I'd be able to make my vows without stumbling and that Ben wouldn't have a paddy in the church or that the crown wouldn't topple from my head—that there wasn't really time to be self-conscious.'

'*Eccellente*,' he murmured, his hand smoothing down over her bare bottom. 'If a queen is self-conscious it does her country no favours. If, for example, she becomes obsessed with her image and her appearance instead of her country's needs, then her role as consort is compromised.'

'Thanks,' she said, wondering if that was supposed to be a compliment or a warning.

The pressure of his fingers over one buttock increased by a fraction to become a warm squeeze 'And how was *this*?' he questioned softly.

She knew exactly what he meant this time but was curious to know how he would phrase it. 'This?' she echoed. 'Perhaps you could be a little bit more specific.'

'The consummation of our marriage vows.'

It was possibly the most cold-blooded way he could have described it but, since she had asked the question, there was no one to blame but herself. 'It...' Melissa swallowed. 'It was perfect. You know it was.'

'Really? You mean there's no room for improvement?' he teased.

'I didn't say that.' She rolled over, leaning on her elbow to look at him, knowing that the first night of a honeymoon was special. That this was the night when, traditionally, words of love were exchanged. But what had Casimiro said to her that very morning? *I hardly think we're a shining example of traditionalism.*

So what would he say if she told him that women loved men for all kinds of reasons? They loved them even when they probably shouldn't have loved them in the first place. He would probably turn round and say that nobody could possibly 'love' after those few passion-filled days which had been nothing more than time out from their normal lives. But he would have been wrong—and every woman in the world would testify to that. Just as every mother would admit that you never really stopped loving the father of your child; for how could you?

And what would he say if she confessed that she could still love him if only he would give her half a chance? That she wanted to love him, if only he'd let her.

Perhaps kings never really let anybody close. Maybe the only way he would ever let her get close to him was in the purely physical sense. So couldn't she just settle for that?

'I think there's plenty of room for improvement,' she whispered. 'In fact, I think we could start improving right now.'

And he groaned as she bent her head and began to kiss the shadowy hollow at the base of his throat.

CHAPTER TEN

THE following morning—feeling a little self-conscious from lack of sleep—Melissa stood on the steps of the villa as Ben arrived in a small fleet of cars, accompanied by Aunt Mary. He gave a little shout as he launched himself at his mother and clung to her neck but it was with a pang that Melissa realised she didn't recognise any of the clothes he was wearing…and that made her feel even more disconnected from reality than her blissful wedding night had done.

'Who bought him that suit?' she asked her aunt as she carried him inside.

'Oh, wait till you see—there's a whole new wardrobe for the little fellow,' replied the older woman. 'Which he'll have grown out of before he can possibly wear all of it. I do hope it won't go to waste, Melissa,' she added anxiously. 'There are plenty of babies in the world who really need new clothes.'

'Oh, I think you'll find we are not so profligate as to squander babies' clothes, Mary,' came Casimiro's wry comment as he walked into the salon, and Melissa saw her aunt sinking down into a deep curtsey.

'You don't have to keep curtseying to Casimiro, Aunt Mary!' she protested.

'Oh, but I do—and I want to,' said her aunt firmly. 'I'll be back in the supermarket aisles on Monday wondering if I dreamed the whole thing—and anyway, it's just respect. And tradition.'

'You'll find that Casimiro has very strong views of traditionalism,' said Melissa, holding the mocking gleam of his golden glance.

'Indeed I do. Speaking of which—do you know that your niece didn't curtsey when we first met, Mary?' he murmured. 'In fact, her very first words to me were: "Go away".'

Melissa shot him a beseeching glance, aware that her aunt's face was wreathed in smiles at what must have sounded like a fond lover's memory—and how misleading was *that*?

'Mu-mu-mu-mu-mu!' babbled Ben, clearly feeling ignored and choosing just this moment to grab a fistful of Melissa's hair and to tug on it as if he were training for a career in bell-ringing.

'Say hello to…to…Daddy,' she said, aware that she was blushing and aware how bizarre it sounded. But what else could she say? The King? His Majesty?

'I would prefer Papa,' said Casimiro, as if he had read her thoughts.

Papa. It was only a little thing—but it wasn't a word Melissa was used to. 'Of course.'

Casimiro turned to Mary with an urbane smile. 'You will stay for dinner, I hope?'

'Thank you, but no, ' said Mary. 'Much more of this and I might get a bit too used to it. I'm flying back to England this afternoon—I can't get out of my stint on the hospital book trolley *that* easily!'

Melissa felt an unexpected wave of sadness as she hugged her aunt goodbye and had to gulp back tears as the four-wheel drive disappeared in a cloud of dust down the snaking track. She stood there watching until it was completely out of sight, looking up to find Casimiro's thoughtful gaze on her.

'She can come and stay any time she likes, you know,' he said softly.

'Unfortunately, she's not really used to a lot of flying.'

'But she'll get used to it.'

Melissa nodded. 'I guess,' she said quietly.

He wondered if the reality of how curtailed her life would be from now on was sinking in at last—and how she was going to deal with it. There was also the question of how he was going to deal with the tousle-haired baby in her arms, who was looking up at him with fearless eyes. And Casimiro held his son's gaze, his own slightly more troubled. Would he learn to know him, and to love him—as all fathers did their sons?

Amber eyes a shade lighter than his own were studying him intently and Casimiro suddenly realised that babies and children were no respecters of privilege or position. That they cared about who you were and not what you represented. Yet countless other men must have dealt with this kind of situation before. How had they coped?

He looked down at the child's small limbs and tried to accept the somewhat unbelievable idea that one day this little creature would be as tall as he was.

'Can he swim?' he questioned suddenly.

'No, of course not!'

'Then I'm going to him teach him.'

And despite Melissa's protests that thirteen months was much too young, Casimiro set about doing just that. A bodyguard was dispatched to purchase several sets of water-wings from heaven only knew where and Melissa realised with a start the subtle extent of her new husband's power. Water-wings or palaces. Private planes or diamonds. Didn't matter what it was—whatever the King wanted, the King got.

Yet as she watched Ben splashing around in the turquoise waters of the infinity pool, being lifted aloft by his powerfully built father, she couldn't dampen down the faint spark of hope which began to flare inside her. For hadn't that image been what she had always dreamed of? That Ben should have a father of his own—and a hands-on father, too? And perhaps learning to know and to love Ben might make Casimiro more approachable—so that he might lose that sometimes icy air of detachment which could be so intimidating.

She was nervous about their first proper shared meal as a family that night—but Ben was so overawed at being waited on and so worn out by swimming and by the presence of this interesting new adult that he behaved impeccably. No food was dispatched anywhere other than in the direction of his mouth. He even ate a sliced banana with a dexterity which made her glow with pride. Nothing whatsoever ended up in the King's lap.

To Melissa's surprise, Casimiro even volunteered to help at bath-time and she had to hide her bittersweet pleasure as she watched him wielding a little plastic watering can and tipping it over the baby's head. She thought how *ordinary* he seemed—laughing as Ben splashed him with warm water—but there was an additional benefit to having a man around, she realised.

Although her aunt had been a fantastic babysitter, this was Melissa's first real experience of sharing child-care and it made such a difference to a mother's life. It was the little things which meant so much—like being able to dry her hair without Ben trying to swipe the hair-dryer. Or being able to shut the door when she visited the bathroom.

She felt almost shy as she waited each night for her new husband to return from reading Ben a goodnight story, and shyer still when his fingers grazed over her skin. One evening, as he played idly with her breast, her hand began to tremble so much that he plucked the half-drunk glass of champagne from her fingers and put it down.

'I don't think you want this, do you?'

'Not…not really, no.'

'Then let's go to bed.'

'We can't keep missing dinner.'

'We can do whatever we want.'

'No, Casimiro,' she said firmly. 'Actually, we can't. The cook has gone to a lot of trouble to prepare a honeymoon feast. Tonight, let's eat first and *then* go to bed.'

He raised his eyebrows in a challenge which was only half mocking. 'Are you ordering me around, Melissa?'

'Not at all. I'm saying what you know happens to be right.'

Unexpectedly, he laughed at her outrageous remark, unused to the sensation of being overruled by anyone—let alone a woman. Somehow he endured a dinner he could have easily forgone—though he couldn't miss the smiles of delight bestowed on her by the staff who waited on them during the meal and concluded that Melissa had been right. But knowing that only seemed to increase his desire, so that by the time they reached their suite he could barely wait to undress her before he lost himself in the welcoming warmth of her soft body.

'You made me wait,' he declared unsteadily.

'Aren't you used to waiting, then, Casimiro?'

'Never.' But she was very good at resisting him, he realised—for hadn't she refused to make love with him in her apartment back in England? And didn't such proper—and unusual—resistance only make her surrender all the more exquisite? So that tonight she seemed to be composed of honey and silk—sliding through his fingers with slick sweetness.

Never had his exploration of a woman's body seemed so thorough and complete. Her soft moans only increased his own pleasure—his orgasm shuddering on and on and on so that it felt as if she had stripped him bare... on every level. And later they lay there as moonlight streamed in and turned their bodies silver, his fingers locking lazily in the glossy tendrils of her hair.

By his side, Melissa stirred. 'Are you awake?'

'Mmm.'

'You were...are...absolutely brilliant with Ben,' she said softly.

'Am I?'

'Yes.' She turned onto her side and stared into his face, touching her fingertips to the dark shadow of new growth at his jaw reflectively. Tonight she was determined that they would talk, maybe get to know each other on a deeper level during that soft, quiet time after making love. 'Casimiro?'

'Mmm?'

'What was your relationship with your own father like?'

There was a pause. Was it the wine he'd drunk with dinner or the proximity of her silken flesh which made him answer without first weighing it up? 'Businesslike,' he said.

'That's a funny word to use.'

'Not really. Things were much more formal in those days. We—Xaviero and I—weren't encouraged to show any outward kind of affection. At least, not towards our father.'

Her eyes widened. 'No hugs?'

'Definitely no hugs.' Hugs were seen as needy. Weak. 'We learnt lessons from our father—hugs we got from our mother.'

'But then your mother died?'

Casimiro's mouth tightened. Why the hell was she interrogating him like this? 'That's right.'

'Oh, *darling*.'

The way she said it disturbed him. Just as the way she touched his face disturbed him. Was it because her actions and her words were coated in sympathy and the last thing he wanted or needed was that—especially from someone who was still brand-new to all the constraints of royal life?

He wished that her naked breasts weren't pushing against his chest because how the hell could a man think when a woman was as unknowingly provocative as this one? And hadn't he better teach her now that he wasn't intending to subject himself to amateur analysis sessions every time they had sex? That peeling back the layers offered nothing but pain and then more pain. 'I'm tired—and you must be, too. Go to sleep,' he said, almost roughly.

But Melissa's night was restless and haunted by insubstantial but faintly threatening dreams and when she awoke the following morning Casimiro was standing by the window—already dressed in a pair of faded jeans which hugged the muscular length of his legs and a T-shirt which kissed every taut sinew of his torso.

Some dark and unknown emotion in his face made her wonder if she'd done something wrong and Melissa sat up, brushing her tousled hair back from her face. 'You're...you're up very early.'

Casimiro nodded. Her lips were kiss-crushed and her eyes looked as green as grass in the morning light. Glossy brown hair tumbled down over her naked breasts and each tiny rosy tip seemed to invite him to take it into his mouth...

But Casimiro silenced the clamouring call of his body. He had found her tender—no, *prying*—questions more than a little unsettling. Because somehow it seemed all wrong to break the habit of a lifetime and allow anyone to get that close—and she needed to understand that. She must be under no illusion that he was intending to share such confidences with her night after night—for what good would that do when the past was dead and buried, and best left that way?

'I have a few things I need to deal with before breakfast.'

'Things?'

'King things.'

His lips curved into a mocking smile but beneath the sardonic humour Melissa could sense his unmistakable detachment. As if a faintly forbidding presence had inhabited the body of her husband overnight—so that this morning he seemed like nothing more than a familiar *stranger*. And suddenly she found herself longing for the man who had opened up his heart to her.

She leaned back against the pillows, telling herself that a woman on her honeymoon was surely allowed to be a little bit provocative. 'Can't it wait?'

Temptation hit his blood like a warm storm spattering over dry rocks. But somehow Casimiro resisted it—telling himself that he *needed* to resist it in order to shrug off the sudden rawness of his senses. Instead, he touched the tips of his fingers to his lips and mimed blowing her a kiss. 'Later,' he promised.

Then he was gone—leaving Melissa lying back against the bank of feather pillows, not only aching with frustration but feeling very slightly foolish, too. A woman having to ask her husband to come back to bed with her and then having her request refused on their honeymoon was pretty shaming. And she found herself wondering if this was how it was going to be from here on in.

Yet he joined her and Ben in time for a late breakfast and afterwards suggested taking them for a walk up the hills behind the house and she looked at him with hope flaring in her eyes.

'But what about Ben—how will he manage?'

'I'll carry him, of course.'

And that was exactly what he did—despite Melissa's reservations about whether or not Ben would design to be carried for such a long walk. Or, indeed, whether Casimiro might flag beneath the child's sturdy and sustained weight. As it happened, neither of these eventualities occurred and the day went perfectly. So did the next—and the one after that. At least, that was what she kept telling herself. Trying to convince herself that it was true when deep down she knew that something was different and she couldn't put her finger on what it was.

To the outsider, Melissa knew they would appear to be having as perfect a honeymoon as was possible, given the unusual circumstances. She had seen the quick smiles of approval from the staff when the King lifted his baby son high onto his shoulders or coaxed him to eat a piece of watermelon at breakfast. She also knew that no new bride could possibly complain about what took place in their marital bed every night. Because even Melissa—with her complete lack of experience of any other lover—realised that Casimiro was a textbook lover. Maybe that was the problem. A textbook lover wasn't a *real* lover, was he? You could go through every permutation of sex possible and you could make a woman shudder in your arms again and again and again, but...

Melissa stared out at the sapphire of the distant sea. Somehow she couldn't stop herself comparing the man Casimiro had been in the past to the man he was now. She tried telling herself that the person who held her night after night was far more real than the lover who had drifted in and out of her life during that rainy summer.

So why didn't it feel that way? Why did their snatched affair feel more real than this honeymoon—and more honest? Was it because back then he had been there by choice, rather than necessity, as now? She wondered if she was imagining the distance which seemed to be growing between them—had she done something to offend him? But when she asked him he gave her a cool and faintly surprised look—as if he didn't have a clue what she was talking about. Leaving Melissa to wonder what life was going to be like when they returned to their royal life back at the palace.

Their last dinner at the villa was delicious and they drank champagne the colour of honey which tasted as dry as a bone. And afterwards, Casimiro dismissed the staff and carried her upstairs to the vast bed where they had shared so many intimate moments over the last fortnight.

'Our last night,' he murmured as his lips whispered a soft path over one soft cheek.

'That's right.'

He kissed away the faint frown at her brow. 'You are sad at leaving?'

She wanted to tell him that the only thing making her sad was his refusal to let her get close—but wouldn't that spoil their last night? 'A little,' she conceded diplomatically. 'It's been…it's been a wonderful honeymoon, hasn't it, Casimiro?'

'Of course.'

She stared at him, her heart beating fast. 'I'm just a bit nervous about what's going to happen when we get back. I mean, how the hell do I go about being your Queen?'

His hand found the silken mound of her small breast. 'You will have plenty of help, *cara*.'

'From…oh, Casimiro!' She swallowed, trying desperately hard to concentrate, but it wasn't easy when he was flicking his finger against her nipple like that. 'From you?'

He gave an impatient little click. 'Not from me, no. There will be a whole host of people to advise you, Melissa—but let's not talk of it now, mmm? Not when there are so many more satisfying things we could do in bed.'

She succumbed to his lips and his fingers and the irresistible thrust of his body because it seemed that was what she was programmed to do. And she waited for words of love which never came—and consequently bit back her own.

When they arrived back at the palace, Casimiro went off for a meeting with his staff while Melissa tried to settle Ben into his nursery after a dinner which ended up mostly over him and on the floor. But he grizzled all through bath-time and couldn't even be placated with a tune from his old plastic mobile which she'd brought with them from England—even though it looked slightly shabby and out of place in his smart new palace bedroom.

She waited for Casimiro to appear, but there was no sign of him and she didn't want to go looking around the still-unfamiliar palace or asking one of the many staff where she should be. Or where dinner was. But there was no way she was going to sit in a formal dining room eating on her own while her husband was nowhere to be seen.

She supposed she could lift the phone and ring to ask for something to be sent to their rooms—like room service in a posh hotel. But she wasn't really that hungry and, besides, what could she order? She didn't even know what the national dish of Zaffirinthos was! Well, tomorrow she would hit the Internet and the library and start learning all about her new home and life. As Casimiro had said—there were plenty of people to teach her.

And tonight?

Tonight she would put away all her stupid and name-less fears and prepare to greet her husband in the most traditional way known to all new brides...

Drenched in perfumed oils, she splashed around in the deep, sunken bath in her huge bathroom and afterwards slid on a green silk nightgown with a matching peignoir which felt as fine as gossamer against her scented skin. And then, picking up a novel whose world seemed in-finitely less absorbing than her own did right now, she settled down to wait for Casimiro.

She waited until ten before wandering into the smaller of their three sitting rooms—where she turned on the television in an attempt to feel normal. But the array of films held as little allure as her book and watching the news bulletins from the rest of the world only increased her feelings of isolation.

At ten-thirty she tried his cell phone—but it was switched off.

By eleven she had fallen into a fitful sleep and when eventually she felt his naked body slip into bed beside her, she opened her eyes to see that the luminous dial on the face of the clock read almost midnight.

'Where have you been?' she questioned sleepily as his hand moved round to cover her silk-covered breast.

'Shh.'

'Casimiro—'

But he was now rucking up her silk nightgown and cupping the globes of her bottom—his skin cool against her bed-warmed flesh as he skated his palms over them with a skill which soon had her trembling with anticipation. Pushing her hair aside to kiss the nape of her neck, he blatantly pressed his hard body into hers so that she was left in no doubt about how much he wanted her.

His silent and sensual onslaught continued to filter through her still-dreamy state and she just let the feelings grow. His fingers found her honeyed slickness and touched her there until she was gasping his name out loud in frustration and need. And only then did he turn her over and pull her towards him and wordlessly thrust deep inside her as his lips found hers.

She came almost immediately—already her body was growing accustomed to the pleasure he could give her—and his fingers tightened around her breasts as she made a soft little cry against his shoulder. She heard the escalation of his breathing—the sudden urgency of his movements and then that distinctive little moan which shuddered on and on.

But once that floaty, dreamy feeling had left her Melissa remembered the long, empty evening she'd spent—without even a phone-call from her new husband.

'Casimiro?'

'Mmm?'

'Where have you just been?'

'Inside you, *cara*,' he murmured, and tightened his arms around her. 'Or hadn't you noticed?'

In the darkness, she blushed. 'That's not what I mean and you know it.'

Fractionally, he loosened his grip on her, and yawned. 'Just what *did* you mean?'

'What have you been doing all evening?'

'I had a stack of paperwork a mile high to tackle.' There was a pause. 'I *have* just been away on my honeymoon,' he added softly.

'I know.' But she could tell that he was being evasive and she could not hold in the faltering little sigh which seemed to come from the very bottom of her lungs.

'You're tired. It's been a long day.' He pulled her against him and smoothed her hair. 'You need to sleep and so do I. Goodnight, Melissa.'

He said it in a kind way. But it was the way in which you might speak to someone who wasn't terribly bright. It was dismissive and it was kindness cloaked in steely control—and Melissa had never felt more patronised in her life.

CHAPTER ELEVEN

'WILL you be back for dinner?' The smile on her face was fixed and bright and beneath the table Melissa's fingers twisted the napkin in her lap as the butler poured Casimiro another of the inky little coffees he favoured in the morning. 'It's just the two of us tonight. Nothing in the diary for once!'

Casimiro glanced up from his study of the pages of the *Zaffirinthos Times* and shrugged. 'I will try, *cara*, but I can't promise anything. I have wall-to-wall meetings with ministers all day—and later I am due to visit the naval base and will stay for cocktails on the new freighter afterwards. So if I'm not back then just carry on without me. Don't bother waiting.'

Don't bother waiting. Melissa's smile didn't waver even if she felt one of those faint flickers of rebellion which had become increasingly frequent of late. Because didn't those few words perfectly capture the very essence of a royal marriage which was little more than an empty shell? A forced union with a man who ticked the boxes as being a perfect lover and part-time father. *And one who displayed all the emotional depth of one of the marble statues of his ancestors!* She twisted the napkin a little more, knowing that it was a better outlet for her frustration than biting her nails.

She was trying her best to be upbeat and mostly she succeeded—even though it had been a baptism of fire settling into her new role. Royal life was certainly packed and—although she had known that every single second was accounted for—she had not expected it to be such a challenge.

There had been balls and tea parties with visiting ministers and dignitaries to meet—each engagement requiring a different change of clothes and a briefing about each person who would be introduced to her. And she'd been given a list of charities so that she could decide which of these she planned to support as patron.

Had this constant pace—this social merry-go-round—been one of the reasons why Casimiro had been so close to abdication when she had reappeared in his life? *The abdication which had never again been mentioned—as if the very real prospect of it happening had been nothing but make-believe.* Every time she had attempted to bring the subject up, she had been stonewalled by a cool censure delivered in an icily aristocratic tone by her husband.

Melissa took a sip of coffee—trying to tell herself that her feelings of inadequacy and confusion were understandable. No transition from commoner to Queen was ever going to be straightforward, but when you factored in that she had borne the King's child, in secret—well, that made the people of Zaffirinthos view her with understandable curiosity. *Will she make our King happy?*—their eyes seemed to say, and Melissa wanted to tell them that, yes, she would—oh, she would—*if only he'd let her.*

And that was the crux of the matter—he just wouldn't. All too quickly she'd discovered that Casimiro had been independent for too long to allow anyone to get really close on a normal daily basis. Isolated by an accident of birth which had placed the crown on his head, he seemed supremely comfortable with his own company.

Deep down, she didn't have a clue what was going on behind the beautiful golden mask of his face. A lifetime of protocol had taught him the most effective methods of blocking unwanted questions and making those questions feel like an intrusion, so that in the end she gave up asking.

Sometimes it felt as if her life with him consisted of a series of formal engagements, punctuated by meals or receptions. Where she would see him seated on the opposite side of a room or a table—unless hers was a solo engagement, in which case she didn't get to see him at all.

And, yes, he still played with Ben—but all the routine of the close father-son relationship they'd forged on the honeymoon had evaporated. These days he saw Ben only on *his* terms—while she ended up feeling like the lowest priority of all in his life.

Only in the bedroom did she ever feel his equal—even if it was purely in a physical sense. There he would kiss her. Cajole away any concerns with the soft caress of his fingers before she had a chance to air them. He would lift her up in his arms and make her feel all woman as he brought her down slowly onto his aching shaft. Melissa swallowed as vivid erotic recall flew into her mind. You wouldn't need to be experienced to realise that Casimiro was an exemplary lover and that she was the most fortunate of wives in that respect.

So why did it increasingly seem as if it wasn't enough? Why, despite Ben's obvious happiness and her own material comfort, did she sometimes feel emptier than she'd ever done in her tiny little apartment back in England? Was it because there at least she'd known who she really was, whereas here…

Here she felt as if she were a ghost of a woman who had chased an illusion, wanting it to be something else—only it had turned out to be an illusion all along.

But Casimiro had never pretended to be anything else, had he? He had warned her off emotion and she had stupidly carried on hoping and hoping that things might some day change. Nothing was going to change—or, rather, he wasn't. He wasn't about to turn into a different man overnight—the kind who discussed everything with his wife, who confided all his thoughts and hopes and fears. Who wanted the kind of close-knit and warm relationship she'd secretly longed for. He was as closed off as he'd ever been maybe *because he didn't know any other way.*

And Melissa was slowly coming to realise that nothing is going to change unless she *made* it change.

Putting down her half-eaten piece of bread and honey, she looked at him across the breakfast table and forced a smile. 'Can't I come too?' she questioned suddenly.

Realising that he was going to get no more reading done, Casimiro put the paper down. 'Where?'

'On your visit to the naval base. I could bring Ben

along with me—I'm sure he'd love to see the big ships.'

He dropped a lump of sugar into his coffee and stirred it. 'That won't be possible, I'm afraid. It's much too short notice—and it's not really a suitable trip for a baby.'

'It isn't?'

'Not really, no.' He sipped his coffee. 'Anyway, it would be wasted on someone of Ben's age.'

'I suppose so.' She tried to keep the frustration from her voice but it wasn't easy. He was missing the point completely and she found herself wanting to slam her cup down onto the table. To tell him to stop being so calm and so polite and so damn *reasonable* and to really open up and *talk* to her!

Casimiro saw the way her lips were pursing up and the memory of how they had whispered over certain parts of his anatomy during the night made him adopt a more conciliatory tone. 'Anyway, you have your own diary, *bella*—certainly enough to keep you occupied. And your own programme of visits.'

Aware that she was being fobbed off, Melissa nodded. 'Yes, I know.'

'How are you getting along with your lady-in-waiting?'

'She's lovely.'

'And the nanny? She meets with your approval?'

Melissa sipped her coffee. She had baulked against the idea of having child-care—jealously wanting to have Ben all to herself. And wondering guiltily if she could justify having help when she wasn't going out to work. But she had quickly worked out that she was being unrealistic and that she couldn't really manage without help. 'Sandy's lovely, too—in fact, all the staff are.'

'So what's your problem?'

Was that how he saw her simple request to accompany him, then—as some kind of problem—when all she wanted was to show him how the quality of their lives could be improved? That if they did more stuff together then perhaps they might start getting closer. Well, he was never going to know unless she told him and time was very precious—especially when you had a baby who was fast becoming a toddler. If they weren't careful, then Ben would be halfway to being grown-up, with two parents who barely knew one another.

'You haven't taken Ben swimming for ages.' This time her smile was wide. 'And he'd so love to splash around in the big palace pool with his papa.'

A pulse began to flicker at Casimiro's temple. 'I think I told you,' he said evenly, 'that I have employed the best swimming teacher on the island to do that—all you have to do is pick up the phone and they'll be ready to start.'

Melissa stood her ground. 'But it isn't the same, Casimiro.'

'No, you're right—it isn't.' He smiled. 'Good though I am, *mia cara, I've* never actually won a gold medal at the sport.'

Her lips curved into an answering smile, but it didn't dint her determination. 'Ben needs to see you.'

'And he *does* see me.'

Something in his implacable face made her growing frustration begin to splinter and the words flew out before she could stop them. 'Yes, he sees you—but it's always on your terms and only on your terms, isn't it? For a few minutes in the morning and a few more snatched minutes in the evening. The occasional lunch at the weekend—if he's lucky. A bit of a tickle and a bit of a play but it's all so...so *snatched*. He's...'

She willed her thudding heart to slow and looked at Casimiro with appeal in her eyes. 'He's at a wonderful and impressionable stage of his life, darling—and he just adores it when he's with you. But if it doesn't happen often enough, then I'm afraid that you're never going to...well, to *bond* with him.'

Casimiro put down his coffee cup. '*Bond?*' he repeated scornfully, but he could feel a cold kind of dread begin to wrap itself around his heart. As if she had pushed him to the edge of a cliff and were forcing him to look down, into the unknown. Starkly it reminded him of those raw feelings he'd first experienced when his mother had died—the ones he'd blotted out. And again when he'd awoken from his coma and everything familiar seemed to have been turned upside down. How dared she? How dared she try to tell him how to run his life when she was a novice to all this?

'I'd prefer it if you kept all your psycho-babble out of this,' he iced out repressively. 'Perhaps when you've been around a little longer, you will understand that this is not the way we do things around here. This is not the way of Kings.'

Something in his imperious attitude made Melissa's fingers stop pleating the crisp napkin—and suddenly she realised that this needed to be said. *Had* to be said. Maybe it would clear the air or maybe it would make things worse but she had to try. For Ben's sake—and maybe for their sake, too.

'A way of life you obviously hated so much that you were about to reject it by abdicating,' she said quietly.

He looked around the vaulted breakfast chamber—the huge windows open to the fragrant drift of blooms just outside. 'Keep your voice down.'

'But nobody's here,' she said softly. 'Nobody to hear but you and me.'

'I don't care,' he snapped.

'But I do. And we've never really talked about it before, have we?' she continued, as if he hadn't spoken. 'The subject was never open for debate.'

'The subject is closed. Finished.'

'But you can't do that. You can't veto something just because it makes you uncomfortable, Casimiro! Otherwise things just build up and up inside you. And then they explode.'

They were about to explode right now if she was not careful. He pushed back his chair. 'I don't intend discussing it.'

'No, that's right. You don't discuss anything, do you?' she questioned in frustration. 'You act like nothing has happened and yet so much has. Because of Ben, you've been forced not only to remain as King, but to marry me—and not once have you ever told me how you feel about it. But then, you don't "do" feelings, do you?'

'Melissa—' he said warningly.

'I haven't finished.' She cut through his objections, ignoring the growing look of fury which had made his eyes flame like golden fire. 'You didn't bother warning your brother that you were about to abdicate in his favour, did you? Without even asking him whether he wanted the position.'

He froze. '*What* did you say?'

She shook her head. 'It doesn't matter.'

'Oh, but it does, Melissa. Really it does. If you have been spending your time engaged in idle speculation on my brother's thoughts—'

'I wasn't *speculating*!' she shot back defensively—and then the words tumbled out before she could stop them. 'Catherine told me.'

There was a long and disbelieving pause.

'Catherine told you?'

'Yes. She said that Xaviero thought you were about to do something dramatic. And let's face it—you were.'

'So you have been gossiping behind my back with the Princess?'

'There you go again!' she accused. 'Shooting the messenger! We weren't *gossiping*, as it happened. We didn't sit down and talk about it—just that when we were out choosing my trousseau she mentioned they'd been slightly worried that you were thinking about abdicating.'

'And you told them that I had?'

'No, of course I didn't.'

'There's no "of course" about it,' he flared. 'Why didn't you give me this information beforehand?'

'Maybe I couldn't see the point, since it was no longer relevant. Or maybe I was worried that I'd get just this kind of reaction,' she said bitterly. 'Autocratic, overbearing—'

'Overbearing?' he echoed ominously.

'Well, why didn't you bother discussing it with

Xaviero first? Were you so certain he'd want to be King? So keen to take on the life you wanted to reject?'

Casimiro stared out of the windows to the gardens beyond without really seeing the bright beauty of the flower-beds. Yes, there had been times when his younger brother had envied him—because the heir to the throne was always singled out as special. But Casimiro had envied Xaviero, too—for the kind of freedom that he as King would never know. Each had wanted something of what the other had.

'For many years, yes,' he said slowly, almost to himself. 'He did—especially as a boy.'

'And lately?'

Casimiro did not know about lately. The new-found weight of the monarchy had driven all personal relationships from his life so that Xaviero had become almost like a stranger to him. But hadn't that happened with just about everyone from the moment the crown had been placed on his head—leaving him in a powerful position of complete isolation? Wasn't that the only way that a King could properly govern his people—by taking full responsibility for his kingdom? 'He did an excellent job of being my stand-in when I was ill,' he answered. 'And if I hadn't recovered then he would have continued to rule. According to my aides, he settled into the job happily.'

In spite of the tension which hung over them like a heavy storm cloud, Melissa couldn't dampen down the flicker of hope which flared inside her. Because this was more than he'd ever admitted to her—and even though she ran the risk of angering him with her persistent line of questioning, wasn't it better to see it through and to thrash it out? Together. To let Casimiro see that she was someone he could confide in. Because that was just as important a facet of her role as visiting schools and opening new roads.

'Wouldn't it have been easier to have sat down and talked to him about it?' she probed gently.

His eyes narrowed as he considered her question. Had it been arrogance which had stopped him from doing just that—or pride? Fear that his memory loss would be discovered—and make him appear vulnerable? Or was it the fact that he and Xaviero never really talked very much? Men didn't; not in his world.

He looked at Melissa now—at the eagerness on her face as she tried to delve beneath the surface despite his repeated warnings not to—and he sighed. She was a good mother and a pleasing lover and she had all the potential to be a great Queen. But that did not give her carte blanche to behave as if she were still living her life back in England. He would not tolerate her interference—and neither would he tolerate her springing things like this on him over breakfast. Far better that she learned that if they were to have any kind of amicable marriage, then she was going to have to learn to follow *his* rules. Rules which had existed in his family since they had first conquered this fertile kingdom, and which had been passed down through generation after generation.

He rose to his feet. 'I don't subscribe to the modern habit of dragging up the past and putting it under the spotlight—I think I told you that on our honeymoon,' he gritted out. 'What's done is done and has no relevance on our lives now. So let's just leave it at that, shall we?

And I'm warning you, Melissa—that this is your last chance. That I cannot and will not have a rerun of this conversation just to satisfy your curiosity.'

Melissa flinched. It was as if she'd been peering into the first few pages of an open book—a book filled with beautiful pictures and a wonderful story—which told her something about her husband's inner life and the feelings he hid from the world. But now it felt as if he'd just slammed that book shut in her face and then flung it to the floor. Her lips parting in shock, she stared up at him in disbelief. His face was hard—a beautiful golden mask, behind which his eyes were cold and forbidding. And a terrible sense of foreboding whispered over her as she recognised that they had reached an impasse and that maybe he needed to know that.

'And I'm telling you that I can't live like that,' she whispered. 'That if our marriage carries on in such a…a *sterile* environment—then it probably won't last, because nothing can grow in that kind of atmosphere. And one of these days I might not be here when you return from one of your trips, Casimiro.'

There was a long, dangerous pause as he studied her. 'That sounds awfully like an ultimatum, *cara*,' he observed softly.

She bit down more of her qualms even though something in the quiet flame of his eyes warned her off saying any more. And yet how could they have any kind of relationship if she was not true to herself? 'I'm just telling you how I feel.'

'And I'm telling *you* that I will not be held hostage to emotional blackmail!'

He saw her flinch and for one moment Casimiro

stared into the bright green glimmer of her eyes, at the brimming tears which smote at his conscience before he resolutely silenced it. Because it was preferable this way, he told himself grimly, and the sooner Melissa accepted that he would not be swayed by tantrums and tears—then the better it would be for them all.

He left the breakfast room, slamming the door behind him, and Melissa just sat there for a long moment, staring at the empty space where he'd been. Waiting until the awful pounding of her heart had quietened. Then she went to find Ben—her spirit heavy—feeling as if the weight of the world had settled on her shoulders. But although she clutched her son tightly to her chest, the misgivings left in the wake of that bitter argument refused to budge—leaving all kinds of fears swirling around in her head. Had her challenge to Casimiro about his behaviour broken the already tenuous thread which linked them, she wondered—and where the hell did they go from here?

Her diary was empty for that day—when she would have gladly valued the distractions of some queenly activities—and instead she threw herself into her role of mother. She took Ben swimming in the outdoor pool and then did some drawing with him—even if he was still at the stage of not really being able to hold a crayon properly. He needed some friends the same age, she realised—and wondered if he was going to be restricted to purely aristocratic buddies or whether he would be allowed to mix with ordinary children.

But her heart was still full of nameless fears and she felt stifled by the palace—as if the walls were crowding in on her, as if the building itself had outed her as some kind of interloper. *You're only here because you have given birth to the King's son*, it seemed to say. And wasn't that the truth?

When Ben went down for his nap, she told Sandy that she was going out for a walk and that she wouldn't be long.

But Melissa did not follow any of the rules she knew she should follow. She did not say where she was going—because she had no idea—and she did not tell palace security either. Silencing the voice of her conscience, she went back to her suite and fished around in the back of one of the dressing rooms until she found a pair of jeans and a T-shirt from her old life which she hadn't quite been able to bring herself to throw away.

She stared at them. What a long way away that life seemed now—when she'd only had one pair of jeans and used to hang them to dry overnight on the radiator after she'd washed them. As Queen, she rarely wore jeans, where before she'd absolutely lived in them—and the smart, neatly pressed variety which graced her wardobe these days bore little resemblance to the faded pair she now clutched.

After first slipping on a modest black swimsuit, she put them on—along with an equally old T-shirt, welcoming the oddly comforting feel of the worn fabric before going outside into the fresh air. As she began walking around the grounds she knew so well she remembered her sense of awe when she'd first arrived to help with the ball. She sighed. It was strange, but today she almost felt like the woman who had arrived to help plan the celebrations not so very long ago—and not just because of the way she was dressed. It was as if memories were crowding into her mind to taunt her.

Look, there was the little staff cottage they'd given her—the house where Casimiro had made that cold-blooded seduction after she'd told him about Ben. It stood alone and at some distance from the palace itself and at that moment it seemed to symbolise everything about her own position there.

She knew where the guards were stationed and she slipped out of the complex without anyone noticing, experiencing a heady rush of pleasure as she did so and realising that this was the first time since they'd returned to the palace that she had escaped from the apparatus of power. No butlers. No ladies-in-waiting. No guards. And no formidable husband who only ever seemed to connect with her when they were exploring each other's bodies.

She walked for a good while before setting off down one of the rocky tracks which led to the sea—and although she knew that she was still within the vast reaches of the royal estates, the sense of freedom she felt was liberating.

Down on the soft white sand, she realised she'd forgotten to bring a towel—or a drink of water—and the sun was baking down hard. But she wasn't planning to stay long. Just long enough to pretend that she was simply Melissa again—with all the lack of restrictions she'd once completely taken for granted.

But deep down she knew it wasn't as easy as that. Yes, she could go through all the motions of escape. She could stand on this warm sand and try to imagine what her old self would have said about this opportunity of having a great big beach all to herself. But that old self was gone. Gone for ever—and she could never get her back, no matter how hard she tried. She felt as if she didn't know her new self very well—this *Queen* Melissa—and suddenly she wondered what on earth the future held for her.

But I will not give into self-pity, she told herself fiercely. *Okay, I have a husband who sometimes acts as if he's nothing more than a beautiful, efficient machine—but I have plenty of other things to be grateful for. A beautiful son. Health. Freedom from financial worry.*

Yet despite her determination to count her blessings, Melissa could do nothing about the terrible pain which ripped right through her as she acknowledged the dark centre which lay at the very heart of her marriage.

Peeling off her jeans and T-shirt, she decided to go for a swim, remembering what her darling mother had always told her. That exercise would wipe worry from a troubled mind. But Melissa's heart was still heavy as she walked down towards the deserted shoreline, where azure water lapped onto the fine sand. The sea wasn't particularly cold—but the silky wash as it slid through her toes was irresistible and, slowly, she began to wade in.

Further in she went, the water reaching to her ankles and then submerging her thighs. It made her shiver as it reached her hips and belly-button—and she gave a little squeal as it tickled against her waist, glad to forget her worries for that one brief moment.

And somewhere in the distant sky, she heard the rhythmical clatter of a helicopter.

CHAPTER TWELVE

'AND the Greek government are perfectly willing to negotiate—that is, if you are agreeable to this last concession, Your Majesty?'

A pin-drop silence fell around the polished table.
Suddenly realising that ten pairs of eyes were fixed on
him, Casimiro also became aware that he was being
asked a question. And that he didn't have a damned
clue what the question was. Because for once he hadn't
been listening properly—his attention only half given
over to the contentious subject of fishing rights in a dis-
puted area of sea. His ministers had come to the meeting well briefed, the subject was one with which he was
familiar—and yet although Casimiro had tried his best
to concentrate it had been to no avail.

*Because all he could think of was that stubborn and
outspoken wife of his and the way she had dared to
remonstrate with him over breakfast!*

For a while he let himself remember her stinging
words. Her emotional claim that he didn't 'do' feelings.
His mouth twisted with scorn. What did she think he
was—one of these *new men* who treated every conversation as if it were a therapy session?

Her accusation about not spending enough time with

his son had hit him even harder. He thought of Ben's gurgling little smile. The way his chubby little arms clamped themselves tightly around his papa's neck. Did she imagine that he didn't miss playing and swimming with his son? Didn't she realise that honeymoons were not like real life—and that he would leap at the opportunity to spend more time with Ben if he were not so weighed down by the demands of being ruler?

The ministers were still looking at him expectantly and Casimiro tried to shift the haunting memory of Melissa's bright green eyes and trembling lips, and to play for time instead.

Because something was troubling him and it all boiled down to a simple sense of logic…if he didn't 'do' feelings—then what the hell could explain this bleak kind of emptiness which seemed to have descended on him like a dark cloud?

He tried to shake off the inexplicable gloom by glancing across the table at Orso—knowing that his loyal aide could always gauge the mood of others, and could instinctively communicate to him what that mood was. And there had been many times when he had been grateful for Orso's instinct in the past—when he had been shielding his memory loss from the world.

Yet now he was free of that amnesia—and it had been Melissa who had jogged his memory and made it return. Melissa who had freed him from the burden and the worry about the blankness in his mind. Had he ever thanked her for that? Made her realise how liberating it felt?

Raising his eyebrows, he turned to his aide. 'What do you think about this proposed concession, Orso?'

Orso bowed his head in response. 'You are the King, Your Majesty.'

Casimiro knew that his aide was playing the procrastination card and that this was a term suggesting that the deal should not be sealed today. But for once, he saw beyond the diplomatic shorthand they habitually used. For once, he took the words at face value—and what he saw in them brought him up short, so that he frowned with a mixture of concern and comprehension.

Because, yes, he *was* the King, yet sometimes he felt more of a puppet—his strings jerked by the demands of his people. By their expectations of him and his own ideas about how those expectations should be met. Ideas which had been passed on down to him by his father, who had governed in a very different time.

Yet *he was the King*, he reminded himself again. And his power was absolute. He could rule this kingdom of Zaffirinthos as *he* saw fit—and the monarchy was not set in stone. It was *his*—to be forged and formed as suited him and *his* life. And Casimiro suddenly realised that if he did not embrace the changes which were necessary to take the monarchy forward, then surely the institution ran the risk of stultifying, or dying—or simply becoming a crushing burden which no one in their right mind would want to take on.

And what kind of poisoned chalice would that be to hand onto his own son?

He was about to suggest reconvening the meeting, when they were interrupted by one of the Queen's assistants, her face so wreathed with anxiety and her curtsey so clumsy that Casimiro bit back his instinctive rebuke at the unexpected disruption.

'Yes, what is it?' he clipped out.

'It's…it's the Queen, Your Majesty!'

Casimiro rose from his chair. 'What of the Queen?'

'She has…gone!'

'Gone?' he bit out, unprepared for the sudden chill which iced his skin. 'Gone where?'

'We don't know, sire. All we know is that the Prince Benjamin has been crying for his mother and that the Queen always wishes to be informed whenever he—'

'Where the hell is she?' he demanded again. '*Some-body* must know.'

'She just said she was going out for a walk, Your Majesty.'

'She didn't say where?'

'No, sire.'

With a heart which now felt like ice, Casimiro re-called more of the words Melissa had whispered to him: *I'm telling you that I can't live like that—and one of these days I might not be here when you return from one of your trips, Casimiro.*

Had she meant it? *Literally* meant it? Found him so overbearing and forbidding that she had run away? He felt the sharp tearing of pain and the realisation of what a fool he had been. A stupid, thoughtless fool.

'Send out search parties immediately,' he commanded. 'And mobilise the helicopter. Alert the airport, too. I don't care what you have to do, just find her. *Find* her.' Hands gripping into tight fists, he headed towards the door—his aides and ministers instantly moving aside as they looked at him with fear written on their faces.

He ran into the grounds, his eyes scanning the vast expanse of green lawns—as if expecting to see her suddenly walking towards him. But there was no sign of her—and the nearby whoosh of air as the helicopter began its ascent somehow filled him with a new sense of foreboding instead of providing reassurance.

Uselessly, he watched as the helicopter grew smaller—a small black dot which began to head for the dark sapphire haze of the sea—and Casimiro set out at a run in the opposite direction, when his cell phone began to sound furiously in his pocket.

Snatching it up, he listened in silence for a moment and then his mouth hardened. 'Send the car to me. *Now!*' he ordered tersely, in Greek.

Within minutes, the four-wheel drive came scorching to a halt beside him and Casimiro leapt into the front seat, exchanging no conversation with the driver or the bodyguard other than the clipped order to hurry as they raced along the cliff path.

Overhead, the helicopter was buzzing in one particular spot and as soon as the car screeched to a halt Casimiro jumped out, running to the edge of the jaggedly high cliff—to see the unmistakable vision of his wife wading into the clear blue water beneath.

The fierce, ragged sound he made was a cry—but instead of issuing from his lungs it seemed to have been torn from his soul itself.

'Melissa!'

But the wind must have carried the word away—either that or she was just ignoring it—for she continued to wade into the sea. 'Get rid of that damned helicopter!' he demanded, and as the driver barked instructions into a handset the aircraft began to move back through the sky towards the palace.

Shaking his head as his bodyguard attempted to accompany him, Casimiro began to scramble down the rocky steps—and never had a journey seemed to take so long. Only when he was almost at the bottom did he shout out her name again.

'*Melissa!*'

In the water, Melissa stilled as a new sound disturbed the silence of the day. A shout which sounded louder even than the helicopter which had been circling overhead but which had now flown away. A shout she would never have recognised if she hadn't turned around and seen the tall, dark figure of her husband descending the steep stone stairs which led down to the beach. She narrowed her eyes—wondering if the bright sunshine had conjured up some sort of illusion.

Casimiro?

He was in wall-to-wall meetings followed by a trip to the naval base, wasn't he? But no, the renewed shout was louder still and it was definitely no illusion, for now he had reached the beach and was tearing off his jacket while running across on the sand towards her with the grace and speed of a natural athlete.

Casimiro? She stood stock-still and watched him.

Kicking off his shoes, he moved fast. So fast that Melissa barely realised what he was doing until he had plunged half dressed into the sea and started wading and then swimming. All she was aware of was his hard, honed body ploughing through the azure water towards her.

'Casimiro!' she croaked.

But by then he had reached her, had caught hold of her—effortlessly half lifting her from the water against the water-plastered silk of his chest—his dark face a series of stark and shifting emotions: fear and anger and anguish. So that for a moment it didn't look like Casimiro at all.

'*Che cazzo stai facendo?*' he demanded fiercely, and then when he saw her blank expression, pulled her closer still—his amber eyes burning like flames as they engulfed her in their angry blaze. 'What the hell do you think you're doing?'

CHAPTER THIRTEEN

MELISSA stared into her husband's angry face and met the hot challenge in his eyes full on, her heart crashing against her ribcage in bewilderment. 'I...I was going swimming, of course! Wh-what did you think I was doing?'

Casimiro let out a strangled sort of sigh, which seemed to have been dragged from some dark place deep inside him. 'How should I know?' he exclaimed. 'How the *hell* should I know?'

And suddenly Melissa saw the fear which underpinned his outward fury. The way his aristocratic features looked knife-sharp beneath the blanched colour of his olive skin. 'You didn't think...' Confused thoughts crowded into her head. 'You didn't think I was walking out to sea—about to end it all because we'd had a row?' Now the thoughts became more focused. And her own fury rose up to match his. 'When I have a beautiful little son waiting for me back there at the palace? Do you really think I place so little value on him, Casimiro—or on me?'

He stared down into her green eyes and shook his head, feeling the mad race of his heart against his sodden shirt. 'I wasn't thinking at all,' he said, in a raw voice.

'I was acting on pure instinct.' Some primitive instinct which had made him want to run straight into the sea and haul her into the safety of his arms.

'And instinct demanded that you rush fully clothed into the sea, did it?' she questioned, trying to pull away from him, but he wasn't having any of it, his grip like an iron clamp around her waist.

He gave an odd kind of laugh. 'Just what would you expect me to do, Melissa? When one of your staff burst into my meeting and told me they couldn't find you. That you were gone—only nobody knew where. And that you hadn't even taken a bodyguard with you. This is unprecedented behaviour for the monarch's consort—how was I to know *what* had happened?'

She heard the unfamiliar tremor which shook his deep voice and for the first time Melissa realised that her need to escape had been completely thoughtless. That it had fed the well-founded fears of a powerful man who had always lived his life in the shadow of danger.

'It was never my intention to alarm you,' she said woodenly. 'I'm sorry.'

His fingers bit into her flesh as he held her tighter. 'So what *did* happen, Melissa? Why did you take off without warning? Was it to punish me?'

'To *punish* you?'

He stared at her. Could he have blamed her for wanting to punish him? And wasn't he now forced to confront the truth—no matter how painful that truth might be? 'For my high-handedness,' he said bitterly. 'For treating you as a possession instead of as a partner. For failing to talk to you properly, or listen to you.'

Her heart began to pound. Was this the prelude to

making some kind of unexpected announcement—for telling her that it was never going to work and that he was going to give her back the freedom she so obviously craved? Had her brief flirtation with rebellion backfired spectacularly on her—had he given into the ultimatum he'd accused her of issuing?

Suddenly she caught the blinding flash of light from higher up and realised that they were being watched. And that whatever Casimiro had to tell her, she would accept it with dignity. She *had* to—for hadn't she already tried harder than most women would have done in a doomed attempt to make their relationship deeper than it could ever be? But with the best will in the world, even she didn't think she could accept the end of her marriage being played out in front of an audience.

'You do realise that your security people have got binoculars trained on us? And that we're standing half submerged in water—you dressed only in a shirt and a pair of trousers. And maybe we shouldn't be having this discussion here.'

Glancing upwards, he scowled. 'Maybe you're right,' he said, and then, without warning, he bent and lifted her into his arms and began to carry her towards the shore.

'Casimiro, please. This is crazy—'

'Damned right it is,' he said grimly.

'I'm perfectly capable of walking.'

'And maybe I'm afraid that you just might run off again.'

'Oh, don't be so ridiculous!'

'Ridiculous, am I, *cara*? I don't think so.'

By now they had reached the dry sand, but still he had her in his arms—and her heart was racing with a tumult of confused feelings as she felt her skin sizzling against his wet clothes. 'Look, will you put me down?' she said breathlessly. 'I promise I won't run anywhere. Please.'

'No.' Still holding her, he continued to walk over to where a crop of high overhanging rocks provided a shaded haven beneath. Only then did he lower her gently to her feet, but he stood his ground, legs parted, his body gleaming with droplets of water. Fixing her in the spotlight of his gaze, his dark golden eyes captured and held her. 'So what happened, Melissa?' he repeated softly. 'I want to know.'

But Melissa shook her head, suddenly loath to tell him of all the doubts and fears which haunted her and made her feel so hopeless about the future—for now that the chips were down, it seemed too big a gamble to take. Wouldn't an admission like that make her more vulnerable still? A slave to his imperious mood if he knew that somehow she couldn't help herself from loving him. Hadn't he made it clear from the very start that he was not the kind of man who wanted that love—and hadn't his actions since only driven that fact home?

'Why are you here?' she asked bluntly.

He was aware that she was stalling. Batting back his questions in a way he wasn't used to—for the King always received immediate answers. But not from his wife, it seemed. His gaze raked over her face and suddenly Casimiro saw the apprehension widening her green eyes and an overwhelming sense of remorse filled him.

Still he hesitated, knowing that he had to tell her everything—but how to begin? How did a man start to express feelings when he had done his level best to deny their existence all his life? 'Because I need to talk to you.'

The words sounded symbolic—but maybe that was just a figment of Melissa's imagination. She could hear the rhythm of the waves, but they sounded a long way away—just as everything seemed a long way away at that moment. It was only her and Casimiro thrashing out differences which had always seemed insurmountable—and the bitter truth was that they still did.

She stared at him. 'Why—what have you got to say?'

The coolness in her voice chilled him as he realised that this wasn't going to be easy. That he must bare his soul to her if he was to have any kind of chance for the future—and never had a single action seemed quite so daunting. 'What if I told you that I've been a stupid, unthinking fool—that I've put up so many barriers and risked losing the most important things in my life, which are you, and Ben? And what if I told you that I want to trust you?' he questioned quietly. 'That I've realised we can't have any kind of marriage without trust and I can't bear to watch the growing sadness in your eyes as I throw back everything you keep trying to offer me.'

She shook her head. 'Stop it,' she whispered. 'Just stop it. You don't have to say things you don't mean—just because you think I want to hear them.'

'You believe that?'

Her laugh was tinged with bitterness. 'Can you blame me?' Melissa stared down at the sand so that he wouldn't see the traitorous tears which had blurred her eyes. 'Why should you suddenly have changed?'

The whispered accusation hurt, but he could not deny

its accuracy. No, he couldn't blame her. Not for anything. He thought of how he'd lashed out at her—at how his coldness and his refusal to communicate might have driven her away. Might *still* drive her away.

And as he stared at her bent head he felt a pain at his heart—a terrible tearing pain he had felt as a teenager when his father had fiercely told him that princes did not cry. That he must be dry-eyed as he walked behind his mother's coffin on that cold and leafless winter day. He had vowed never to feel that kind of pain again—to protect himself from its merciless onslaught—and yet he was feeling it now. He recognized now that pain was the price you paid for love. And recognized, too, that a hurt even greater lay waiting unless he could convince his wife that he *was* prepared to change.

He became aware that she was shivering. 'Wait here,' he said tersely, returning just seconds later with his discarded jacket, from which he shook stray grains of sand, and then looped it gently about her shoulders.

Melissa inhaled deeply—she just couldn't help it. Because the jacket smelt of him—his own distinctive scent—all musk and sandalwood and pure, unadulterated male. She felt surrounded by him—cocooned by him—and wasn't that a perilous way to feel?

'Sit down,' he said softly.

Aware that he was trying to cajole her—and she still wasn't quite sure why—Melissa sank down onto the shaded sand and stared up into his golden eyes. 'Okay, I'm sitting down and I'm warm. So why don't you tell me what it is you want to say, Casimiro?'

Casimiro saw the way she had crossed her arms tightly over her chest—in a gesture which unmistakably said *go away*. He wanted to reach out and touch her but somehow he recognised that touch would blur the edges of what he knew he had to say—that he needed to do this without any reliance on the senses.

'When I left this morning I was furious.' There was a pause as he struggled to articulate it. 'Mainly because you had forced me to look at myself and the way I was living my life. Forced me to confront the way I was feeling—actually, the way *you* made me feel, if only I was prepared to let go and admit it. And I realised that if I didn't act quickly, then there was a very real chance that you might leave me and the thought of that rocked the foundations of my world.'

'Casimiro—'

'Shh.' He stared at the faint tremble of her lips. 'I've realised that you were right—that my life has been consumed by my kingdom and that isn't a good thing. Not for me, nor for you—or Ben—not even for Zaffirinthos. I've realised that I have to find a new way to govern—a way which will still allow me to be a good, strong King, but which will also allow me to be a good husband, and father. Because balance is important—to every human being. And I realised that I couldn't possibly let my son inherit a crown that I had grown to resent.'

Melissa looked at him, hardly daring to acknowledge the sudden leap of hope in her heart. 'But…how is it going to change?'

'I'm going to speak to my brother. At our wedding he told me that it had taken a move away to make him realise just how much he cared for Zaffirinthos. I don't know how much is possible—all I know is that I'm going to work something out. Do you believe that?'

'Yes, Casimiro,' she affirmed softly. 'I do.'

Her instant trust made him smile, but it was a smile tinged with the fear of what he might so easily have lost. 'When I found that you'd gone—it was as if my worst fears had been realised,' he continued quietly. 'It made me stop and imagine the reality of a world without you. One with no steadfast smile nor welcoming arms. No tender fingers to stroke and caress my stubborn face in bed at night. And it made me realise that I couldn't let that happen. Couldn't bear for it to happen. Something made me run to find you—the same something which drove me to your door on the night of the ball, when you first told me about our baby. Something you've always been able to arouse in me, Melissa—which defies protocol. The spark of it was always there, I think—even back then in England—but I've only just managed to put a name to it.'

'And what name would that be, Casimiro?' she asked softly, aware that he was at the very edge of something— but needing him to go further. To hear him speak the raw and naked truth so that there could be no possible misunderstanding in the future.

His gaze was steady and yet his hand was anything but. Such a small word and yet surely the most powerful word in any language. 'Love.'

There was a heartbeat of a pause. 'Love?' she questioned lightly—as if it had been a slip of the tongue and she was quite prepared to let him correct himself.

He saw the uncertainty written on her features and the hope which underpinned it despite her determination not to let it. 'Yes, love,' he said softly. And now he *did* touch her—but only to lift the hand which wore his wedding and engagement bands. 'Do you realise that when I knew I was going to have to marry you because you had given birth to my child—a part of me rejoiced at the thought that you would be mine. All mine. That I could see you and have you as often as I wanted.'

'Yet you didn't show it.'

'Of course I didn't,' he said. 'Because I was terrified at the way it made me feel.'

'And how was that?'

There was a heartbeat of a pause. 'Vulnerable.'

'*You*, vulnerable?'

'Yes, me.' With a rueful expression, he looked into her face. 'You see, I've come to realise that I'm no different from any other man, not really—not when it comes to matters of the heart. And that I'm certainly not immune to such feelings, no matter how hard I tried to fight them.'

She reached out to touch her hand to his cheek and he caught it, and kissed it. 'Oh, Casimiro,' she whispered.

'I love you, Melissa,' he said softly. 'I love you for being you—strong enough to stand up to me and strong enough to care for me. I love you for the son you have borne and so lovingly reared—despite the adversity which fate threw at you—and I will love you both for the rest of my life, if only you will let me make up for my stubbornness. My inability to accept what was staring me in the face.'

Emotion was welling up inside her as some lone voice in her head told her she should have protested. She tried telling herself that he couldn't possibly mean it. But Melissa knew not a moment's doubt about

Casimiro's declaration—it was written on every taut feature of his beloved face. And before her, she saw not a King—but a man who had always put duty first. A man brought up by a grieving father, without the soft and loving touch of a mother's guidance. Who could ever blame him for the brittle exterior he had erected around his heart?

She was so moved that it took a moment before she could speak. 'I love you, too,' she said, and tears were now pricking at her eyes—she just couldn't help them. 'I always have and I always will.'

With fingers which still weren't quite steady, Casimiro framed her face within his two hands, shaken by the re-alisation of what had so nearly been lost but now lay within their grasp. And all they had to do was to reach out and take it. 'Can you ever forgive me?' he whispered.

She nodded, touching her mouth to his, absolving him with the tender brush of her lips, swallowing down her unshed tears of joy as she looked into his beloved face. 'It's over. Past. Done. It's the future which matters now—and, of course, the present.'

'You're my present. Such a beautiful present—which I would like to unwrap this very instant,' he said as he smoothed the windswept hair back from her face. 'But since there are lots of men with binoculars in the vicin-ity—then I guess I'll just have to make do with this.'

'What?'

'This.'

He took her by the hand, moving away from the um-brella of the rocks—so that they stepped out into the bright sunshine of the day. And with scant disregard for protocol or the security men who were lining the cliffs above them—the King took his Queen in his arms and began to kiss her.

EPILOGUE

AND that was how the monarchy of Zaffirinthos became a model for the world—with historians and sociologists vying to write endless papers about it. It was seen as a remarkable model—how two royal brothers, both with pretty large egos, could manage to share power so successfully.

In talks which had taken place over several weeks, Casimiro had persuaded Xaviero and his family to move back to the island and for his brother, the Prince, to take on a significant role there. Though, as Melissa pointed out, it didn't really take much persuasion at all. Xaviero loved his land and had begun to miss it—just as Princess Catherine had learned to love it. And they both wanted to bring young Cosimo up on its shores. They had both tired of London and hungered for the pure blue light of the Mediterranean, the quietness and the calm of island life.

The younger royal couple moved into the villa on the eastern side of the island—to the magnificent mansion where Casimiro and Melissa had spent their honeymoon. And Cosimo and Ben began to play together on a daily basis. It was good for both boys to have company, Melissa recognised—and even better was the fact that, when the time came, they were both going to attend the island nursery school instead of having private tutors. A new generation of royal children had been born and their whole way of life would be different as they moved into a new age. They would be taught that duty need no longer take precedence over love.

Melissa insisted that Casimiro speak to the doctors about his amnesia—especially since he had now confided in his brother what had happened. And, to her darling husband's astonishment, the doctors had been laissez-faire about the revelation. He was given a clean bill of health and told that temporary amnesia was fairly common in serious head injury.

'You see?' she teased him in the car, on the way back from the new children's rehabilitation centre which they had just opened together—as they undertook many of their engagements together these days. 'Everything is much better when it's out in the open!'

Casimiro smiled. At the hospital, he had gone on a spontaneous visit to the intensive care unit where he had almost died. It was the first time he had been back there—and yet he had derived a strange strength from seeing the stark white beds and all the high-powered equipment once more. More than anything it threw a light on what was most important in life. And in a life he now saw was blessed, the most important thing he had was his family. His beautiful wife and his beautiful son—who gave him all the love he needed.

And it was all down to this woman, he thought, pulling Melissa into his arms and tipping her face up to look at him. 'Yes, *mia bella*,' he murmured. 'You were right. But then, I think perhaps you are always right.'

'That is the correct answer!' Melissa's smile was impish as she lifted her mouth to be kissed, knowing she could twist her husband right around her little finger—as he could her.

'In fact, did you read that article I left you yesterday?' he queried indulgently. 'The one saying that I looked so happy since my marriage that perhaps you are the power behind the throne. Do you think that is so, *cara mia*?'

But Melissa shook her head as he began to kiss her. No way. There was only one power in their lives today and that was the power of love.

Coming Next Month

from **Harlequin Presents® EXTRA.** Available February 8, 2011.

Coming Next Month

from **Harlequin Presents®.** Available February 22, 2011.

REQUEST YOUR FREE BOOKS!

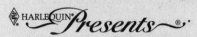 

2 FREE NOVELS PLUS
2 FREE GIFTS!

YES! Please send me 2 FREE Harlequin Presents® novels and my 2 FREE gifts (gifts are worth about $10). After receiving them, if I don't wish to receive any more books, I can return the shipping statement marked "cancel." If I don't cancel, I will receive 6 brand-new novels every month and be billed just $4.05 per book in the U.S. or $4.74 per book in Canada. That's a saving of at least 15% off the cover price! It's quite a bargain! Shipping and handling is just 50¢ per book.* I understand that accepting the 2 free books and gifts places me under no obligation to buy anything. I can always return a shipment and cancel at any time. Even if I never buy another book, the two free books and gifts are mine to keep forever.

106/306 HDN E5M4

Name _____ (PLEASE PRINT) _____

Address _____ Apt. # _____

City _____ State/Prov. _____ Zip/Postal Code _____

Signature (if under 18, a parent or guardian must sign)

Mail to the **Harlequin Reader Service:**
IN U.S.A.: P.O. Box 1867, Buffalo, NY 14240-1867
IN CANADA: P.O. Box 609, Fort Erie, Ontario L2A 5X3

Not valid for current subscribers to Harlequin Presents books.

Are you a current subscriber to Harlequin Presents books and want to receive the larger-print edition? Call 1-800-873-8635 today!

* Terms and prices subject to change without notice. Prices do not include applicable taxes. N.Y. residents add applicable sales tax. Canadian residents will be charged applicable provincial taxes and GST. Offer not valid in Quebec. This offer is limited to one order per household. All orders subject to approval. Credit or debit balances in a customer's account(s) may be offset by any other outstanding balance owed by or to the customer. Please allow 4 to 6 weeks for delivery. Offer available while quantities last.

Your Privacy: Harlequin Books is committed to protecting your privacy. Our Privacy Policy is available online at www.eHarlequin.com or upon request from the Reader Service. From time to time we make our lists of customers available to reputable third parties who may have a product or service of interest to you. If you would prefer we not share your name and address, please check here. ☐

Help us get it right—We strive for accurate, respectful and relevant communications. To clarify or modify your communication preferences, visit us at www.ReaderService.com/consumerchoice.

HP10R

USA TODAY *bestselling author Lynne Graham*
is back with a thrilling new trilogy
SECRETLY PREGNANT, CONVENIENTLY WED

Three heroines must marry alpha males to keep
their dreams...but Alejandro, Angelo and Cesario
are not about to be tamed!

Book 1—JEMIMA'S SECRET
Available March 2011 from Harlequin Presents®.

JEMIMA yanked open a drawer in the sideboard to find Alfie's birth certificate. Her son was her husband's child. It was a question of telling the truth whether she liked it or not. She extended the certificate to Alejandro.

"This has to be nonsense," Alejandro asserted.

"Well, if you can find some other way of explaining how I managed to give birth by that date and Alfie not be yours, I'd like to hear it," Jemima challenged.

Alejandro glanced up, golden eyes bright as blades and as dangerous. "All this proves is that you must still have been pregnant when you walked out on our marriage. It does not automatically follow that the child is mine."

"'I know it doesn't suit you to hear this news now and I really didn't want to tell you. But I can't lie to you about it. Someday Alfie may want to look you up and get acquainted."

"If what you have just told me is the truth, if that little boy does prove to be mine, it was vindictive and extremely selfish of you to leave me in ignorance!"

Jemima paled. "When I left you, I had no idea that I was still pregnant."

"Two years is a long period of time, yet you made no attempt to inform me that I might be a father. I will want DNA tests to confirm your claim before I make any decision about what I want to do."

"Do as you like," she told him curtly. "*I* know who Alfie's father is and there has never been any doubt of his identity."

"I will make arrangements for the tests to be carried out and I will see you again when the result is available," Alejandro drawled with lashings of dark Spanish masculine reserve.

"I'll contact a solicitor and start the divorce," Jemima proffered in turn.

Alejandro's eyes narrowed in a piercing scrutiny that made her uncomfortable. "It would be foolish to do anything before we have that DNA result."

"I disagree," Jemima flashed back. "I should have applied for a divorce the minute I left you!"

Alejandro quirked an ebony brow. "And why didn't you?"

Jemima dealt him a fulminating glance but said nothing, merely moving past him to open her front door in a blunt invitation for him to leave.

"I'll be in touch," he delivered on the doorstep.

What is Alejandro's next move? Perhaps rekindling their marriage is the only solution! But will Jemima agree?

Find out in Lynne Graham's
exciting new romance
JEMIMA'S SECRET

Available March 2011
from Harlequin Presents®.

Start your Best Body today with these top 3 nutrition tips!

1. **SHOP THE PERIMETER OF THE GROCERY STORE:** The good stuff—fruits, veggies, lean proteins and dairy—always line the outer edges of the store. When you veer into the center aisles, you enter the temptation zone, where the unhealthy foods live.

2. **WATCH PORTION SIZES:** Most portion sizes in restaurants are nearly twice the size of a true serving and at home, it's easy to "clean your plate." Use these easy serving guidelines:
   - Protein: the palm of your hand
   - Grains or Fruit: a cup of your hand
   - Veggies: the palm of two open hands

3. **USE THE RAINBOW RULE FOR PRODUCE:** Your produce drawers should be filled with every color of fruits and vegetables. The greater the variety, the more vitamins and other nutrients you add to your diet.

Find these and many more helpful tips in

YOUR BEST BODY NOW

by

TOSCA RENO

WITH STACY BAKER

Bestselling Author of
THE EAT-CLEAN DIET®

Available wherever books are sold!